SHADOWS

D. M. Imbordino

D. M. IMBORDINO

outskirtspress

DENVER, COLORADO

Outskirts Press, Inc.
http://www.outskirtspress.com

ISBN: 978-1-4787-1428-6

Outskirts Press and the "OP" logo are trademarks belonging to Outskirts Press, Inc.

PRINTED IN THE UNITED STATES OF AMERICA

For Shelley,
my dear little sister
we have lost but have never forgotten.
With all my love
until we see each other again.

As I sit alone in these old but memorable rooms,

I remember a place of happiness,

But it is no more.

The walls have collapsed

And its foundations have fallen with Father Time.

All I have left is but memories

of this once happy and joyous place.

It brings such tears to my face.

And no one but I and I alone

Carry these memories of my heavenly home.

Prologue

Suffolk, England

The old woman cradled the phone in her hands as she waited for a voice on the line. The room was small, but big enough for a woman of her advanced years. She kept her direction toward the fireplace, absorbing its comforts of warmth. The fire's embers flickered and pulsated as though they had a life of their own, greedily taking in all the oxygen of their desires. The soft sounds of Chopin played out in the distance on her record player. She listened and felt the music uplift her soul. She let out a soft sigh. She bent her arm, bringing her hot toddy to her mouth, and swallowed deeply. The bitter weather of the land was making her ache. It was the usual weather of the United Kingdom. Her nose ran slightly with the remains of a cold that she could not shake. The woman impatiently spoke out again when no one responded on the phone.

"Natalie, if this is you? It's not funny," the old woman said to the person she thought was her childhood friend.

The caller finally spoke. "Mum?"

She gripped the phone tightly as she listened. She thought she heard the voice of her son but wasn't sure. His tone was distant and quiet. "Hello," she shouted. The connection was horrible. The sound of static took over the line. "Please, if anyone is there, could you speak louder?"

"Mum?" the caller said again.

The softness of his speech made the woman fearful. "Son, is that you? Is everything all right? I haven't heard from you in years. Please tell me where you are."

She thought she heard a slight cough and then him clearing his throat. "It's me, Mum."

Her body was racked with goose bumps and alarm. She could feel that something was amiss. "Where is your family, kid?"

She could hear him sobbing. It was so uncontrolled that she couldn't understand him. "I want to help you, but I can't if you don't tell me where you are," she said in desperation. "Is everything all right? Is something wrong?"

"I am here, Mum. I came back home. I wanted to see you, but I can't. It's too late. My wife is still back in the States."

The woman couldn't shake the feeling of dread, so she continued. "Why are you here without your family, kid?"

"I wanted ..." the crying was back in his voice.

"What, dear? Speak up; I can't hear you. Please tell me what's wrong."

"I wanted to... I wanted..."

The woman heard her mother speaking behind her. "Something's wrong, I just know it. Make him come home, love."

SHADOWS

The woman ignored her mother, trying to listen to the quiet voice on the line. "Yes, kid. You wanted to what? I can't hear you, lovey. Please say it again." She held the phone, waiting for another response.

"I wanted to ... die here."

The woman almost dropped the phone from the feeling of shock. She extended the other hand to reinforce her grip on the receiver. "What are you taking about? What have you done?"

"I can't be with them anymore, Mum. It's too much. The voices won't stop. I had to leave so they would be safe."

"Listen to me. I want you to come home, and I will help you the best I can. Okay?"

The hysteria of the cry began to turn into a sarcastic laugh. "You can't help me, Mum. No one can. I want you to know that I love you. And ..."

"Don't do this to me, kid," the woman pleaded. "You're breaking your mam's heart. Come home, and I will help you. You'll see." The urgency in her voice was heard and understood by the caller.

"And ... I am sorry for everything. I am not strong enough for this. The medication doesn't help. The voices, Mum. You don't want to know what the voices say to me. The things they want me to do. I am no longer in control. My family isn't safe anymore. No one is, around me. It has to end."

The elderly woman didn't like where the conversation

was going. "Kid, listen to me and listen well. You know if anyone can help you, it's me." The woman began to cry. "Please come home. I know I can help," she stated confidently. "I know I can make things right."

"I want to be with the family at Highgate. Mum?" the caller shouted. "Mum, did you hear what I said? Take me to Highgate. Promise me."

"Stop talking like this." The woman stood up, frightened of what she was about to hear next.

"Promise me!"

"I will do no such thing!"

"I need you to understand. I have to go. I need to know that you will do this for me."

"You know what you are asking of me? You know what will happen if you do this? Please don't do this to me. Not now. After all these years, you finally come home to ask this? I can't."

"Yes, you can," the voice said. "It is my last wish that you do this for me. Give me your word."

She was losing the battle; she could feel it in her bones. He had already made his decision. The woman fell back in her chair defeated. As a single tear caressed her face downward, she said with closed lids, "Please come home. You know I would anything for you kid. I know I can."

"I love you, Mum."

She heard a sniffle and some more crying. Nothing could prepare her for what she was about to hear. The explosion from the receiver was so loud that it startled her. She dropped the phone in fright. As the phone dangled on the end of its cord, she could hear nothing else but the phonograph playing Chopin next to her. The music stopped. Then there was nothing left but silence.

Chapter 1

Eleven years later
Ellsworth, Maine

It was early morning when we arrived at the house. As the car approached the cast iron gates, the sun began to rise, giving little hints of its presence over the horizon. Traveling from the sunny beaches of California to this cold, damp, rainy place made my bones ache. I cringed when Mom told us about the move. Some unexpected circumstances led us here to Ellsworth, Maine, twenty-seven miles from Bar Harbor. My name is Amanda Pennington. I am first-generation American, along with my twin brother Toby. My mother, Lauren, was born in a little village called Burtonwood, which is located in the northwest part of England. She is what you would call a starving artist. She had a beautiful gallery in California until her partner, Julian Smith, ruined everything. Mom, the trusting soul she always was, never questioned Julian's activities until the market crashed and the money ran out. Julian owned 51% of the gallery, so he took the profits and threw them into the market for a quick buck. Businesses closed down, people were losing their jobs, and Mom (aka Lauren) found out she was completely and utterly broke. With no family and no help, Mom was at a loss and had to make the biggest decision of our lives. That decision was to move.

I heard her cry in her room for five days straight. As I lay in my bed, staring at the ceiling above me, I could almost hear her inner thoughts. It broke my heart to hear my mom cry. I was only sixteen. What could a kid say to her parent that has lost everything? What comforts can I give?

Lauren was a very tough woman, and we rarely heard her weep, but when she did, it always brought me back to the sad memories of my father, Lucas Pennington. I never really knew him exactly, you see. My father died when I was very young. All I have are little images of him in my mind, along with a memory or two. Nevertheless, it will have to do. It was something, wasn't it? When my father died my brother and I were only five years old. The last memory I have was on the day of the funeral. I don't really know what happened to him. I had heard someone say it was an act of God, whatever that meant. Mom doesn't talk much about my father, and I don't ask, fearing to cause her grief. I have tried to find information on my own, but it's hard, with no living relatives and no starting point. Now it's just us.

When I was growing up, everyone always admired my mother's accent. "Hello, love," she would say, and they all came running. With my mother's career, the British accent made her sound more rich, warm, and inviting to newcomers. The car brought me back to the present as it began sputtering, begging for more gasoline. As I looked up once more, Mom was out of the car, trying to open the unwelcoming entrance. She placed one foot on the gate and left the other planted on the ground as she tugged away.

"Five bucks says she'll be there for at least ten minutes," Toby stated.

After a moment, I replied, "You're on," with an outstretched hand for a shake.

Toby won. She did it in twelve minutes. "Told ya," he said with a knowing smile. "Pay up."

As she pulled the gate, it finally gave in with a loud screeching sound. Toby and I looked at each other in disbelief, and then I said, "By the sound of that, I think it's been a while since this house had visitors." I reached in my purse and pulled out a ten. "Do you have change?"

Before I could get an answer, Toby snatched it and put it in his pants pocket. As I went forward to grab him, Mom called my name.

Mom was wearing a red sun visor, smiling with that cheesy grin. "Sorry it took so long. The gate wouldn't move," Mom stated as she got in the car. The car whined as she put it in gear.

As the car began to move Toby put on his MP3 and placed his headphones over his ears, "I have a feeling we're going to wonderland, Alice," he teased.

"Don't forget you owe me five bucks." I held out my fist for a silent promise as I whispered.

"What did you say?" He started teasingly, "I have my headphones on my head."

I just glared at him.

"Yeah. Yeah. I know, I know. I'll get it to you sooner." He got closer to my face. "Or later," he enunciated with emphasis.

"It better be sooner," I whispered back under my breath. My Siamese cat, Taboo, came between Toby and me a meowed loudly in disapproval of our argument.

The drive to the house itself was about a half mile. By then the sun was shining fully and the house was … well, let's just say that this house was very, very, unusual. Scratch that. Let's go with creepy instead. The Victorian building that was once white had yellowed with age. The wood in some areas was bare and dry rotted. Some areas didn't have any wood at all. The house reminded me of an old abandoned castle. The porch was an expansive wraparound that had a large balcony above it. I am sure in its day it was grand, but the remnants of what once was had been replaced with chaotic disarray. I squeezed my eyes into slits to get a better look.

I saw that the third floor of the house had also a balcony with two trellises beneath it. And the roof. The roof, good grief, where was the roof? Everything about the place was askew. All I could do was look in disbelief. I couldn't believe that this was the place. The walls themselves lacked stability.

"Mom, you've gotta be joking; we can't live here," I stammered. As I said it, I felt a twinge of regret. I got out of the car, closed the door, and leaned on it with my arms crossed in defiance.

My mom slammed the door to close it properly. When it didn't, she bumped the door with the side of her hip until she heard the latch connect. She smiled with satisfaction and walked over next to me, mimicking the same stance. As her brown hair shined in the sunlight, she sighed. "Okay, so it needs a little paint." She moved closer, touching her shoulder to mine.

My eyes nearly bulged out of their sockets. "A little?"

Mom put her hands up like I was attacking her, "Okay, okay, a lot of paint." Mom pulled her visor from her head, and in a tired voice she whispered, "A lot of paint."

Toby got out from the other side and snickered.

"Mom, where in the world did you find this place?" I asked.

"On eBay," she answered sarcastically as her green eyes looked into mine. Our eyes, Toby and mine, were the only things we had from our mother genetically. It was the only hint of our relation to each other.

"Yeah, right, sure. You wouldn't even know how to get on eBay if your life depended on it," my brother retorted.

"A friend of a friend," she finally admitted. "It was a

part of her inheritance." Mom was silent briefly and looked forward. "She said no one has been here for a while and her grandfather left it to her. She asked for only $50,000." She shrugged, "If you ask me, it was a steal. We have ten acres on top of this." She pointed to the house for effect. "The house in California is still on the market. It was all I can do for now until it sells." She hesitated slightly before speaking again. "Besides, I think this will be fun. The house was built in 1850."

Toby and I stared at each other in silence. Mom was waiting for a reaction, and we knew we had to be supportive; besides, we could always get a job and help. Couldn't we? "Great," we spoke out in unison with smiles as wide as our mother's.

Mom smiled again and clapped her hands together, "Great, okay. Well let's have a look inside, shall we?"

We smiled until she was nowhere in sight. Toby leaned in my direction across from the blue Volkswagen Beetle. "Do you think it would hurt her feelings if I said I'll live in the car?"

"Toby," I began as I walked over to the trunk and pulled out a bag, "let's at least try, for Mom's sake." Taboo purred as she walked over to me, grazing against my leg.

I tossed him a garbage bag of his clothes. He flinched as it hit the ground. "I was afraid you would say that."

"Besides, it can't be any worse. Can it?" I asked with a slight hesitation.

Toby headed for the front door. "Let's see," he stated as he disappeared into unknown territory.

I still didn't move. The house was old and needed a lot of TLC. I slowly raised my bag and slung it over my shoulder. A slight chill emerged from inside of me and the hair on the back of my neck rose. In the distance, I could hear a slight rumble, and I cringed. "I had to open my big fat mouth, didn't I? First day here, no roof, and what does it do? Rain." I took a small breath and began dragging my feet to a place I would like to call my personal hell.

I walked closer to the house. I could hear the echoing of my footsteps as I walked on the old cobblestones. When I placed my foot onto the porch, I could hear the boards creaking beneath my feet, crying to give way. Each step seemed worse than before. With each stride it felt as though my very freedom was fleeting; the happiness I once had was replaced with a melancholy solitude within me. "I hope I can at least make it to the front door before I break my neck." I moved slowly, trying to get to the entrance. I placed my hands on the doorknob and pushed it open. The doors creaked and groaned as if awakened from a deep sleep. I moved into the foyer. I turned to the back wall with intentions of turning on the light. The only response was the echoing of the light switch in complete darkness. "Niiccee, it just keeps getting better and better," I said to myself.

"What did you expect? The power isn't on yet," Toby

wailed out from behind me, scaring me senseless.

I dropped my bag in front of myself. "Don't do that," I yelled out, holding my chest.

Toby was leaning against the front doorway laughing. "Oh, come on. I didn't do it on purpose."

I tried to peer deeper inside the room, but my vision still hadn't adjusted to the darkness. The only hint of light was streaming in from the windows. As I focused more, I could see what looked like stairs, but they were in bad condition. They ascended and curved to the right. A section of the stairs and landing had fallen down at some time. It was evident that we would not be venturing upstairs yet.

"I guess we won't be going upstairs for a while," I said as I rubbed my sweaty palms against the front of my jeans. "Where's Mom?" I questioned.

Toby was still in the same place. He shrugged, "I suppose she's somewhere on the first floor," he stated sarcastically.

"Smart aleck."

I left my bag where I dropped it and walked around a bit to get a feel of the place. The floors were all hardwood, but the varnish and lacquer had faded. I turned to my left to the adjoining room. It looked like a family room. A large fireplace was against the far wall. The mantel was made of oak and cherry in color. The design was beautiful. It looked like cherubs with horns outlining the inner hearth. In the front of the fireplace was a granite step that was about twelve inches higher than the floor. At first, it was hard to tell the color was green until I wiped across it with my hand. The fireplace would fit a family of five inside it alone. There were old curtains on some of the windows. They were tattered and worn. They were probably once a shade of green that matched the step. I was surprised to see furniture still in the room. "Very odd." As I raised my sights to the walls, I saw paintings. Of what, I couldn't tell. Years of dust had concealed them. I contemplated why the previous owners didn't take their belongings. I hugged myself, hoping to get warm, but a chill still emanated from me.

I could see that the house still had some charm, but it would take a lot of work. In a way, I could understand why Mom wanted to move to Maine. The area seemed more pastoral and family oriented. California was fun and warm, but maybe Mom wanted quiet and to have her own personal creature comforts. Mom had always talked about getting a big old house and making it her own. In a way Mom was doing what she always wanted to do. She was living her dream. I just wished she had waited a few more years. I always believed that everything happened for a reason. Didn't it?

I shivered again from the breeze that brushed against my back. As I gazed at the large fireplace, I smiled. "I think you are going to show me some warmth tonight." I shivered some more, but it wasn't from the cold. I thought

I felt ... *nah; it's just an old creepy house.*

I walked farther into another adjoining room. It was a library filled with books on the shelves. The bookcases were of a lighter color, like caramel. I walked closer and pulled down the first book I saw. It had a red hardback leather cover. I smiled as I read the title. *Leaps and Bounds*. Holding it in my hands, I looked around the study. "This was a leap, all right." I started to place the book back into its resting place, but I decided to hold onto the book to read for later. I grabbed the sliding ladder attached to the bookshelf and pushed it to see if it still moved. It did with little effort, so I nudged it some more and stood on it for a short ride. I laughed slightly, resting my head against the ladder. I went over to the window to bring more light in, so I opened the mahogany curtains before leaving the room. I went roaming around, trying to find my mother. I stopped for a moment, thinking I heard something behind me. It was probably just the house settling a bit. I tried to brush it off and then kept moving on.

I slowly retreated to the foyer. I didn't like where my thoughts were going. The longer I stayed in the house, the more I agreed with Toby about sleeping in the car. I did find my brother again, still in the position I left him in. I was beginning to think he was thinking the same thing about this place, but I didn't say anything. All I said was, "A storm is coming. We need to find a place in the house where we can stay dry for the night." I looked up to the ceiling. The water damage wasn't as bad as I thought it was. Nevertheless, we were going to get wet. The view of the roof from the outside was horrid. The holes were the size of cannon balls.

We can do this. We can make this work. I closed my eyes and inhaled deeply to remove the stress I felt from within. *We always plunge into things head first. This weekend we will tackle the roof and the movers. Then on Monday,* I thought with a cringe … *SCHOOL.* When Toby still didn't move to find Mom, I figured I would do it myself, leaving all my thoughts behind for now.

Chapter 2

O ur first night here, and what do we do? We ordered pizza. It took the delivery guy forever to get there. I drove down to the gate and stood in the cold, waiting to wave down the car. When a car did stop before me, a window rolled down. On top of the hood was a sign for Pizza Joe's. The driver seemed very surprised to see someone there.

He smiled after his initial shock as he pulled his rusty Cadillac up farther toward me. He poked his head out of the window and spoke out. "I thought it was a joke when we got the call for this address," he shouted to drown out the storm.

I smiled back in return, "No, no joke. We are living here now."

"Sorry," he replied. "I'm Josh," he said as he got out of the vehicle, holding out his hand toward me.

I took his hand in mine. "Amanda."

As he stared at me intently, I couldn't help thinking of how I must have appeared in this weather. My curly black hair clung to the sides of my face, and I was sure that my mascara had smeared.

"All right, Amanda, that will be $25.50," he replied as

he removed the pizza from the car.

I handed him $28.00 and told him to keep the change.

Just when I thought his smile couldn't get any wider, it did. He thanked me and said he'd probably see me around in school. As he got in his car and drove off, I just stared blankly. What can a girl in this kind of weather say to keep a conversation going? I ran back to our car and drove to the house. I wished I had more money to tip him.

I was a bit embarrassed when he asked if I lived here. The house didn't seem very homey or safe. In a way, I felt like I was going to bear the label at school of the freakish girl that lives in the spooky house on the hill. I tried to erase it from my thoughts. When I got closer, I stopped the car and stared into the rearview mirror. I tried to remove the dark smudges from under my eyes. "Figures." I pushed my hair back so I could see better. I hugged my father's coat closer to my body as I shivered. My father's coat was all that I had of him. It comforted me at times, making me feel as though his presence was still around me. I grabbed the pizza box and was thankful that the rain slowed down a bit. I was hoping that I did not slip and fall into the mud.

As I walked into the kitchen, mom removed a few dishes from the cabinet above and tried to wash them under the water tap. I could hear what sounded like grumbling. The faucet, along with the house itself, shook as liquid sputtered and flowed from the faucet. The water must have come from a well, or maybe the pipes were rusty, for the color was dirt brown. The explosion of water splashed up and hit the front of Mom's shirt. She turned off the water quickly and grabbed a roll of paper towels. "I guess we won't be washing dishes anytime soon," she announced jokingly as she dried her hands on a towel. Toby laughed a second and then thought better of it and stopped.

We placed the slices on a piece of paper towel. We sat in the kitchen and quietly ate our grand meal surrounded by candles. The storm was still frenzied. It did not seem like it would ease up anytime soon. The trees swayed, refusing to give and break under the pressure of the harsh winds.

The kitchen was very large. In a way, it reminded me of the high school cafeteria. It was very spacious but cold, with many windows to the outside. This was too much room for a family of three.

The mahogany cabinetry reached up to the ceiling. The doors to all the shelves were made of clear glass. The walls looked as though they were the color of lavender at one time. The wallpaper was peeling downward, exposing the plaster beneath it, showing its nakedness. A large granite island stood between us and the old iron gas stove and a fridge. Above the island, there were copper pots and pans that hung from their handles on a rack. The candlelight illuminated the room, casting shadows against the walls. It was an eerie and gloomy setting indeed. It reminded me of *The Addams Family* show.

Most of the cobwebs were gone, except for those that hung on the chandeliers above us. The depression was setting in, and so was the reality. We were going to live here for a while. I hoped it wasn't going to be very long. A flash of lightning cracked like a whip. The pure brightness of it caught my eye, and the rolling thunder continued to rumble loudly.

I tried to envision myself back at home in seventy-five-degree weather. As I closed my eyes, I could hear the water crashing against the rocks. The damp smell of the sea and the sound of gulls screeching in the upper skies filled my senses. People were lying on the beach, getting brown from the rays of the sun.

Water dripped from the ceiling to the pan below. The drops that escaped the tin pan and hit my feet was the water from the ocean splashing me as I was surfing on that big wave. I tried to imagine that the storm was the ocean, but it wasn't working. I tried harder, but the distraction from the outside was blocking my imagination. The sand beneath my toes, the clear skies, and the blue crystal water were eluding me. The clanging noise of the pan became the music on the beach that blared in the background. This was not working. The vision was fading. I couldn't bear it anymore. All my friends were in California; that life was over. Yes, I was feeling very sorry for myself. This was it for now, and what a strange and ominous place it was. I had to ask the question about this place to Mom that had been plaguing my mind all day, but how do I start? I decide to begin the conversation bluntly. "Don't you find it odd that there are a lot of personal items still in this place?"

Mom stopped her hands just before the edge of the pizza touched her lips. She decided to bite in anyway, before she responded to the question. I waited until she chewed and swallowed. The suspense was killing me.

"No, I don't." Mom waited a moment before adding, "Maybe her grandfather had a personal estate to escape from city life."

"Mom," I stated as I raised my voice slightly, "by the looks of this place, no one has lived here for at least twenty years. Come on." By my Mom's facial reaction, I knew that I was going a bit far.

"I think it's cool," Toby stated as he munched on his own serving.

"You would." I took in a breath.

My mother looked at me. "What was that?"

"Nothing," I responded in frustration. "All I am saying is that it's a bit strange, that's all." I asked, "Where are we going to put the furniture that's here when the moving van comes?"

I flinched when I saw the lightning that flashed in the window, and then I heard a crash of thunder. Boy, that sounded close, too close.

"I guess we could put it in the basement," Mom began, "but I will ask Julie if she wants the stuff."

"Julie, as in the person who sold you this place?" I asked with curiosity getting the best of me.

"Yes, Julie Warwick, okay?" she responded with a hint of irritation. "Look, the house has fallen into disrepair. I knew it would need work, but I was just as surprised as you were."

"Okay. Okay," I answered with one outstretched hand, trying to protect myself from Mom's attack of words.

Mom stood up and began to clean some more. Toby moved closer to me. "What happened to 'Let's make this work for Mom's sake'?"

"Oh, shut it," I replied, knowing well that I had upset her.

I stuffed the pizza in my face and bit forcefully, knowing that I went too far, but I had to voice my opinion, didn't I? Nothing about this place made sense. As I turned my sights to the shadows, once again I thought I heard a small noise. I saw a door open slightly. Out of curiosity, I stood up and walked toward it. I grabbed the flashlight off the island to see what I could find. As I opened the door slowly, a small smile appeared on my face. "Bingo!"

Toby ran beside me to see what I had found. "What?"

As he peered around the door, his gaze followed my flashlight inside. To our surprise, there were another set of stairs, and they went up. Mom came over to investigate for herself. As she slung her arm around me, her curious stare drew her inside. She took the light from my grasp, and she raised the beam upward to get a better look. A slight breeze caressed my face, bringing a musty smell to fill my nose. The cobwebs lined the stairs in their own design. A cold draft from the secret entrance engulfed us. I shivered and rubbed my shoulders in a circular motion. We stood for what seemed like an eternity. For me, five minutes seemed like infinity. The storm still continued in the background, making its own music. I felt weary and excited at the same time to see what wonders were hidden inside. I felt like Jim in the *Treasure Island* storybook. I was a young adventurer that wanted to find all the answers. Mom drew me from my thoughts.

"Great, we have a decent pair of stairs." Mom's eyes closed into slits, trying to see farther up. "They look like utility stairs. The servants used them in the old days to bring the food up to the owners and their guests."

I was the one to ask, "Can we go up and see what there is to see?"

The flash from the window caught my eye again, and I turned to look at the outside storm.

"I am going up first, just to make sure it's safe," Mom said as she disappeared into the darkness.

For some odd reason I could not wait to investigate the upper level. In a way, it was a bit exciting. I think at the time it was more curiosity than anything. It would be a perfect ending to a dreary night. Maybe there was a bed, a big soft bed with plush sheets waiting for me. At this point,

I was so tired I could sleep on the hardwood floor. It was a long way to travel in a car across the United States. A nice warm bed would be my salvation indeed.

I could hear Mom shuffling upstairs, and then all was quiet.

"Mom," I shouted. "Mom," I yelled out again.

Mom's face appeared before my own. "I hear you just fine," she yelled as I jumped. "The floors seem safe enough. You can come up, but for just a minute. Please, let's stay together."

Toby and I ran to the kitchen counter. I grabbed extra flashlights from one of Moms bags. We came back, grinning with excitement and followed Mom up the stairs. The second floor was cool. At some point, I lost Mom as I wandered around the hall. I don't know how it happened. I stopped paying attention, and somehow lost her. I went down the wallpapered hall to the very last room. The thing that attracted me to this room was that the door was closed, as if hiding its secrets within. There was a heart etched in the center of the oak panel. It looked like there was writing on the door. I touched it lightly, trying to see what it said, but it was too faded to make out. Maybe this house wasn't such a bad idea after all. The door seemed appealing and inviting. Maybe we did need something new, but I still missed home. After a failed attempt to read the inscription on the door, I turned the handle and crept in.

The room was empty but big. There was a large bay

window at the far wall with a velvet window seat. This room was toward the back of the house. I walked closer and sat on the dusty seat. As I plopped down onto the cushion, the dust flew into the air, making a cloud of dirt. I laughed aloud and looked out the window as I began coughing. To the right was a large trellis attached to the side of the house. I closed my eyes and smiled, "Roses, red roses." Satisfied with that thought of what I was going to plant for the trellis, I gazed to the other side. To my surprise, there was a small balcony. I opened the broken glass doors and figured I would peek outside. For the first time since I had been to this place, I liked what I was seeing. The storm was breaking and the view was breathtaking. The trees were still a lush green, and the sky was all different colors. I could hear the birds chirping in the distance. I inhaled the misty air and closed my eyes. Yes, this would definitely be mine. This room had my name written all over it.

I stepped back inside. I removed my flashlight from my father's jacket and moved back into the hallway. "Toby," I said. When I tried to turn on my flashlight, it wouldn't work. I hit it sharply with an opened hand as I said "Toby" again. I shook it hard as I stepped forward into the darkness. "Mom, are you still upstairs?"

I heard someone step behind me, or at least I thought I did. That's when I quickly turned around. I didn't realize that from the storm, the hallway floor was soaked with water from the leaking roof. I moved too fast, losing my footing. I fell in the darkness, and that is all I remember, falling, falling, falling.

I opened my eyes to see a pair of brown eyes staring back into mine. His face was stern and filled with seriousness. He came closer. I was lying on the floor a bit disoriented and confused. I felt his cold hands as he picked me up and walked into the bedroom, to the window. He placed me on the purple velvet window seat and gazed at me once more. He then lifted one side of a seat, revealing a secret compartment. He pulled something out from the window seat. It was small and square. It looked like a small brown jewelry box. He opened it, hiding its contents from me. I thought I heard a music tune briefly before he closed it. It sounded familiar. The melody was soft and humble. It reminded me of one of those songs that a mother would sing to put a child to sleep. The room was vibrant and alive, as if it had a life of its own. The dull colors were replaced with a blue velvet hue. I was trying to regain my bearings as I began to stand, but he pulled my arm downward in a silent warning for me to sit again. He looked older than I did. His high cheekbones enhanced his facial features and gave him character. His large overcoat seemed slightly outdated, but in a way it suited him. I started to feel scared, not seeing any sign of my mother or Toby.

I could hear the distant voices below and laughing, but I couldn't make out what the others were saying. A bright light surrounded him like a blanket. I didn't notice it before. Why was he here? I tried to peer around him to see where the source of light began. He stopped me from looking and regained my attention.

I tried to speak to him. "Thanks."

He cut me off with a sound of silence, making a slight shushing noise.

I looked down as he raised his closed fist to me. When I tried to speak, he silenced me again when his index finger touched his lips in a silent signal of quiet. He opened his palms up to me so I could see what he was holding. It was a small silver box in the shape of a heart. He started to open it and turn it around so I could see what was inside. As he moved it closer to my visage, I opened my eyes wider to see, but the vision seemed to fade.

"You have to leave," was all I heard in a slight whisper, and then he was gone.

"Dad?"

I opened my eyes to find myself sprawled on the hallway floor. Holding my head in my hands, I moaned aloud.

Mom ran to my side in distress and concern. "Amanda, what happened?"

I rubbed my head again where the goose egg started to reveal itself. I winced when I felt the sharp pain. "I don't know," I replied as she helped me up. "I must have slipped on the water on the floor."

Mom looked at me as if I was crazy. "What water, love? I don't see anything on the floor over here."

I looked down, baffled and in denial when I saw nothing but a dirty floor. "I don't understand. I thought——" I did not get to finish when Mom spoke up.

"Maybe you thought you slipped on water, honey. There is nothing there. You must have had a bit of water on your shoes from when you were outside."

Still holding my head, I said, "I was out on the terrace a moment ago."

As I pulled my hand away, I saw the blood, and then I felt a bit dizzy. That was when Toby came to us from out of the darkness.

"What happened to you?" he questioned as Mom held me up, looking at my head.

"I don't know. I fell, I suppose."

Toby shook his head in disbelief. "It figures, you're so accident prone, Amanda."

Mom started speaking into the crown of my head as she looked down to see the damage, "I don't think you need stitches, but I think I should take you to the hospital to make sure."

Mom helped me walk downstairs and sat me down in the kitchen chair while she inspected some more. She then left briefly to get some towels from a box and brought them over. She started to apply pressure on the wound to get it to stop bleeding.

"Mom, I am okay. I don't need to go to the hospital." I took the towel from her in embarrassment and anger. "See,"

I stated as I pulled the towel away. "It's almost stopped; it was just a soft spot I hit, that's all. I don't want to go to the hospital."

Mom gave me a stern look and then responded, "I think we should get it looked at."

"*Mom*."

"All right." She put her hand up to silence me. "I don't want to hear one more word. Get in the car."

Great, first day in this old house, and I get hurt. Toby watched me from the back seat as Mom drove to the hospital. "You know, Amanda," he began, "you might have to get one of those tetanus shots. You may have caught yourself on a rusty nail." His smile indicated that he was hoping I'd get it.

I threw my bloody towel at him so he would just stop talking. "I don't need a tetanus shot."

"I don't know, Amanda, a tetanus shot sounds like a good idea."

With the storm and Mom not being familiar with the area, it took her some time to find the hospital. She then remembered that she did in fact have a GPS to locate one. As we pulled into the drive, the sign said Main Coast Memorial Hospital. What a day!

Chapter 3

Monday finally arrived after the big fiasco of the week-end. Mom wanted me to stay home for the day. I fought her all the way, insisting that I go to school. She was worried that I may have had a slight concussion. I didn't want to go to school; believe me, education was not my number-one priority. I just wanted to get away from that house. It made me feel uneasy. Toby was the same about it. It was our first day of Ellsworth High, home of the Eagles. It was a different school, but they never change. Every place always seemed the same. It was always similar stories and the same atmospheres. There were the jocks, the preps, the cheerleaders, the Goths, the gangsters, and the eccentrics. Where did I fall in theses categories? I was mixed somewhere in between them all, having my own sense of style. Okay, it's called no style at all. Blue jeans and a faded T-shirt was me. The very fabric defined me. A plain look attracted the least attention. My dark, long, curly hair had a mind of its own. Today it was uncoopera-tive, so I put it up in a ponytail. I preferred it that way. It also kept the stitches on my head from being visible to others.

I was just there to get by, like most. College was not

something I wanted in life. At sixteen, who knew what they wanted to be? I was still trying to find myself, not figuring out an occupation for later in life. It was a small town. I laughed aloud sarcastically and then stopped. I hoped no one was listening to me. I did hear of smaller places. When we lived in California, there was a town called Tupman. The joke was that if you blinked, you would pass the community. The only problem with small communities was that everyone knew your business. Nothing was secret or sacred, as I was soon to find out. The pizza guy, aka Josh, was in fact Joshua Salisbury, the quarterback of Ellsworth High. He did not hesitate to let the other kids know that I was coming. Some were welcoming with open arms. Others were cruel and relentless, especially when they found out where I lived. It was as I feared it would be. I was labeled Amanda, the teenage psycho that lives in the Victorian Queen Anne house on the hill. I went with it the first day, avoiding the scrutiny as much as I could. I ignored most and retreated within, listening to my music.

Every teacher liked to introduce me to the entire class, which was a nice thought. If teachers would only inquire if new students liked to be introduced. If you ask me, any student would like to remain unseen. My literature teacher, Mr. Mann was the one staff member that I liked the best. He only said my name once and never asked me to come up in front of the class and to tell them something about myself. The less I talked, the better. The student body already had a tainted idea about my character and me because of my new residence.

At lunch, I decided to sit alone. The menu for the day consisted of rice and chicken, or my favorite, meatloaf. Yummy. Of course it isn't my favorite, but my choice of the day. I was always a meat and potatoes kind of person. Oh, who am I kidding? Give me a candy bar any day.

Unlike most teenage girls, I didn't care about calories or carbs. Just feed me and let my metabolism do the rest. I guess in a way I was lucky. I was only one hundred fifteen pounds. I continued listening to my favorite tunes as I slowly chewed away on the rubbery delight. I was surprised I had not seen my brother. Our schedules were different. What surprised me was the fact that we didn't share one class. I guess it was fate that we didn't even have lunch together. Unlike most siblings, my brother and I were close. We got along better than most.

I pulled my sweatshirt tighter to myself. I didn't like Maine's weather much. I needed heat. I even missed the sounds of those pesky gulls that flew overhead. I checked my cell phone to see if I missed any calls from old friends. There was one text message from Madeline Drew, my best friend. She even sent me a picture of the group. I missed them. I wasn't a popular kid at the old school, but at least I was happy. Mom say's I am young and I will adapt. That remains to be seen.

The melody playing through the headphones brought

back a memory from when I was five. It was when mom went back to the UK to bury my dad with his family. We stayed in a little inn outside the village. I recalled it most because the only bathroom was in the hallway that all guests had to share. That was unpleasant. In a way, Maine reminded me of the atmosphere from my mother's country. Maybe that was another reason for her coming here. It brought her closer to home, but she said we could never go back. I never understood why. It was the first and last time Toby and I were ever there. I remember distinctly that we had one visitor after the funeral, but my mom hesitated and told me it was an old friend. The older woman didn't seem to be a friend. When my mom ushered the stranger outside, all I could hear was loud mumbling sounds from the window. I didn't understand one word of the conversation. When I asked who she was, Mom changed the subject. I believe that over the years Mom thought I had forgotten about that day. To be honest, I did until this very moment. The bell rang out, signaling that lunch was over. Pulling myself up, I grabbed my tray to dispose of what was left.

Art was an all-time favorite of mine. NOT! I couldn't even draw a stick figure correctly. Today was pottery day. The teacher, Mrs. Cline, assigned the class to make something that would reflect ancient Egyptian times. The hard part was to recreate what we saw in the picture. I only hoped that I didn't create a monstrosity. The best part of class was that Joshua Salisbury was in it. At least there was some scenery to look at. How was I supposed to know that the pizza guy would be him? I should have known better; after all, it's just my luck. I have none. Never did. The slow dripping of the rain was putting me to sleep. I could feel my eyes slowly drift upward under my lids. I shook myself awake twice, hoping that sleep wouldn't overcome me. It was the last class of the day. I only had ten minutes left.

I looked away from the clock when I heard my name.

"Amanda."

I directed my eyes toward the teacher with a blank stare. "Yeah?"

The teacher remained silent, and a person or two in the classroom giggled.

I tried to compose myself and asked, "I am sorry, can you repeat the question?"

"Can you come up and tell the class a bit about yourself?"

After a few giggles from the class, I stood and complied as asked.

"What is the secret of life? SURVIVAL."

I keep telling myself that high school should be the best years of my life. At least that's what others keep telling me. I hated freshman year at the old school, but I still had my friends. Junior year here will be a challenge. I sat in the back of the bus and contemplated my situation. The drive home was harsh. I could feel every bump. A sharp pain shot through my spine. The heat wasn't penetrating the back of the bus efficiently, either. Choosing the last row wasn't a smart decision. I stood up, staggering to the front to find warmth and comfort. When I sat down again, a little voice beside me drew my attention.

"Hi."

As I turned my head to follow the sound, there sat a fellow student. At least I thought she was a high school student. She had the height of a ten-year-old kid. To be nice I said hello in return. I couldn't be rude, but of course when I wanted silence, the girl took my greeting as an invitation and started a conversation.

"I am Daphne."

"Amanda."

"You're the new kid in town that I heard about."

"Guilty," I said with my right hand up.

I thought *Here we go with a hundred and one questions.* They didn't come. That surprised me. Instead, I got information.

"I heard you bought the old Warwick place."

I just shrugged in response.

Daphne pulled her large glasses down the bridge of her nose to get a better look at me. "No one stays there very long. That house has a very bad history."

"I am sure it does," I responded in a sarcastic tone.

"No, you don't understand." Daphne scooted closer. "I am always at the library researching. You should go there sometime and take a look."

"What do you know about it?"

Daphne smiled, knowing she had gotten my attention. "Your home and land around it is responsible for two hundred ninety-three deaths."

She had my undivided attention. "Seems like a pretty big number."

"One person went missing and was never found." Daphne nodded her head to me in certainty.

"Was it only the Warwick family that owned it?"

Daphne shook her head from side to side. "It originally belonged to the Eaglestones."

I was drawn deeper into the conversation.

"The Eaglestone family was the first to settle in this area. The name means *dweller at the eagle rock*. That is why our school's mascot is an eagle. Not many know that."

I knew better than that. "Ellsworth was settled in 1700s. The house was built only in 1850."

"That's true, that's very true. But what was there before that?"

"Excuse me?" I stammered out.

"There was a house there before that one. In 1850, your house was rebuilt over the old one. Some portions of the house encase the original timbers of the other structure. Ellsworth back then was called Sumner. The Eaglestone family was one of the first; many came afterwards."

"What happened to the Eaglestone family?"

"They all died. No one knows exactly of what. Small pox, maybe. The Wabinaki believed that the piece of land you live on was evil. The story goes that the Wasichu, otherwise known as the white people, were welcome to stay. They didn't tread on the land where you live."

I stared at Daphne, dumbfounded. "You are very informative. You sure know your history."

"I know a lot about your house. Everyone does. Not very many will go near it. One psychic said that the house was unclean."

"What did she mean by that?"

Daphne looked up. "It's your stop."

The bus driver stared at me impatiently through the rearview mirror.

"Oh, I guess I'll see you tomorrow." I walked off the bus and then stood at the sidewalk.

Daphne laughed, "Maybe not," she screamed out the window as the bus passed by.

When she said those words, it gave me a chill. That girl was weird but harmless. I turned my sights to my new home. My breath turned into a misty cloud from the frigid temperatures and rose slowly upward. Toby wasn't on the bus today. Mom must have picked him up for some reason. With an intake of breath, I passed the gates and walked the half mile uphill to the house on Water Street. The house might have a horrible past, but it was just a house. Wasn't it?

My thoughts were back on the night I fell. I shook my head, thinking I just hit my head too hard and it was just a weird dream.

I decided to walk around to the back door, entering into the kitchen. There I found Toby with a rag on his face.

"What happened to you?"

Irritated, Toby said, "Fight."

I placed my book bag on the island as I moved closer to him. "Why did you get into a fight?"

"I don't want to talk about it, Amanda. Mom's mad enough as it is."

"Are you suspended?"

"If I want to live another day, I better not be."

"What was it about?"

"Guess," he replied with a small amount of venom in his voice.

He didn't have to tell me. I knew how it was today myself, with all the teasing. At least I didn't lash out.

"What did the principal say?"

"Nothing much. She saw that I didn't have a record in any previous school. I guess she wasn't surprised when she saw who else was involved."

"Who was it?"

Toby took the cold rag off his face and looked at me. The shiner was starting to reveal itself. It had a slight blue tinge to it. I winced when I saw it.

"His name is Nathan Simms."

"That looks like it hurts." I moved forward to touch it.

"Ouch. What are you doing?"

"Reminding you what pain feels like. Payback for that little hint that I was past due for a tetanus shot. Does it hurt?"

"Of course it does," he shouted with a sarcastic laugh.

"It was bad enough I needed stitches. I didn't need a shot to go with it."

I reached out, teasing Toby. I wasn't going to touch it again though.

"MOM!" he screamed out.

"Oh, don't be such a big baby." I leaned on the island across from Toby and cupped my face in my hands. "Did you at least get in a good shot?"

"You figure it out."

"Did you hit him first?"

Toby dropped the rag from his face again and gave me a cold stare. "Yes, but he did put his hands on me. He pushed me." He shrugged. "I hit him. End of story."

"And his minions came running along, itching to join in and commence the beating of Toby."

"Something like that, yes."

I shook my head in disbelief. "You better come up with something better than that, or you are toast."

"It's the truth."

I eyed Toby down, waiting for him to recant his story.

"Is she really upset?"

"What do you think?"

"No. Really, how mad is she?"

"Mad enough to ground me for the rest of my life. She took everything out of my room, even the video games. Now what am I supposed to do in this place?"

"Well." I crossed my arms in front of me. "You could always get back on her good side and start fixing things around here. You were always good with that stuff. Besides." I shrugged. "She'll save some money on top of it."

When Mom came into the kitchen, she didn't speak a word. She grabbed her keys in anger and walked to the back door. She mumbled something about going to work at the gallery in the center of town. I didn't even know she had found a job so soon.

I whistled out loud and turned back to Toby. "Yep, she's really mad at you. You better start working out your penance."

"So, besides my day, how was yours?"

"Peachy," I responded quickly.

He bowed his head. "As bad as mine, I take it."

I ran up the utility stairs two at a time and walked quickly to the room that I claimed as my own. After a brief moment of hesitation, I walked over to the window seat and pushed the cushion upward. As I looked into the compartment, my curiosity turned into utter disappointment.

It was empty.

Chapter 4

Two weeks after we moved in, things were coming together slowly. Mom found a roofer in town that was
going to charge her only $8,000 for the job on the house.
It was the cheapest she could find. I couldn't wait to have a
dry home. I slept on the second floor for the first time last
night. Mom wanted us to still sleep on the first floor, unsure of the soundness of the floor boards, but reluctantly
she gave in to my nagging. It was a bit breezy last night. The
soft howl of the wind was actually soothing. I slept soundly
without a care in the world. No dreams or strange visions,
just darkness. I still wondered about my fall. The vision
still plagued my mind. Was it my father I saw? I couldn't
be sure. The mind had a funny way of working at times.
When I woke up I actually felt pretty good, yet I still didn't
want to crawl from the warm bed. I placed my bare feet
onto the cold, wooden floor and gave a quick intake of
breath. It was like stepping on ice. I quickly recovered and
adjusted to the temperature difference. Before I stood up,
I looked to the window seat, hoping that I would see my
father again, but he wasn't there. A twinge of disappointment filled me.

I walked over to the window while putting my robe

on. The bright red fabric undulated as it formed around me. I tied the belt on my midriff before I sat down on the faded seat and looked out the window. It was beautiful. The leaves on the trees had started the color change that occurs with the changing of the seasons. The sky matched the landscape, giving off little hints of colors like the rainbow blending perfectly in its own design. I wished I could paint. If I could, this would be the inspiration to place on the canvas. This was a great beginning for the day. I opened the window and inhaled the morning air, hoping for energy for the day's events. After a great hesitation, I got up to get ready.

I walked down the utility stairs. Toby was at the base, waiting for me. Toby wasn't suspended, but still had to go to school looking like a bus had hit him. It surprised me that my mother had not spoken a word about it. If it was me, it would have been worse. It wasn't fair. We made our lunches side by side and then started our way outside.

A carpenter showed up in the early morning hours to start fixing the stairs and landing in the front of the house. With my backpack slung over my shoulder, I said a quick hello and walked with Toby to the bus stop. Things had seemed to quiet down, and I hadn't had another strange episode since that first night here. I kept it to myself. I did hit my head pretty hard. The sun was still in its silent slumber leaving us still in darkness.

Bus 78 finally made the trip down Water Street to pick

Toby and me up for school. As we moved through the bus doors, I looked up. I didn't see Daphne. Toby and I sat together in the back in silence and traveled the ten miles to school. Toby's face didn't look as bad as it did a few weeks earlier. The bruises had faded and the cuts had healed. I looked at him before we got off the bus. I held out my closed fist to him. He closed his in return and touched his fist to mine.

"Behave today, Tob."

He smiled in response to my suggestion. "Of course I will. Don't I always?"

I nodded, knowing full well that Toby always finishes what he started. I just worried how far his antics would go. Toby was not the sort that just left well enough alone. When Toby was messed with, he would retaliate again and again. But Toby was always the sneaky sort that didn't get caught. When he did things, he planned them out well before actually doing them. I just sat back and waited for the magic to unveil. I was sure before the school day was out I would see something. The whole school would. In a way, I felt bad for the Simms boy, for Toby at times could be straight-out evil, but it wasn't like the kid didn't deserve it. Toby at times portrayed himself as a modern-day Robin Hood. The bully always got his when it came to Toby.

I shrugged it off and began stepping down from vehicle 78. The sun was bright now. Placing my sunglasses my face I smiled knowing well that I wouldn't regret coming to school today. I dressed casual, as usual. Jeans and a black sweatshirt was the choice today. I placed my bag inside my locker and began moving to the classroom. At least no one stopped me in the halls. I guess the news traveled quickly and had gotten old already. It was good enough for me.

"Hey." I heard I shout from behind.

I guess I was wrong.

I looked to see who had shouted. I saw little Daphne trailing behind, holding a handful of books in her arms. I just smiled and turned around, trying to get to my class.

"Hey," I heard her say behind me. I looked again. "Didn't you hear me?" she asked, short of breath.

I smirked in response. "Yes, I heard you." I pointed at the clock as we passed it in the hall. "I am trying to get to class."

Daphne looked hurt. "It's only homeroom."

I pulled my books tighter to my chest. "I didn't see you on the bus this morning."

It was Daphne's turn to smile. "Missed me?"

"Hardly." I chuckled. "Daphne, what do you do for fun?"

"Excuse me?"

I knew she heard the question. "You know, fun. Does anyone have that around here?"

Daphne pushed her glasses up the bridge of her nose. "I like the library."

"So you've said," I interrupted her boldly.

Daphne was beginning to think. "A lot of the kids hang out at the lighthouse on the coastline of Mount Desert Island."

"Really?" I was taken back. "What is there to do at a lighthouse?"

Daphne shrugged. "I never go there with other kids, but I'll tell you, you've never seen a lighthouse quite like this one."

"It doesn't sound fun."

"Believe me, it can be, or so I've heard." Daphne decided to change the subject drastically. "How's living in the house?"

I gritted my teeth, "Quiet."

"Really?"

"Yes."

"More like dead quiet?"

"Daphne, is there any other kind?" I arched my brow at her.

Daphne laughed. "You're okay."

The bell rang for homeroom, and I was late. "Thank you again, Daphne; conversation with you is never dull."

"I live to please," she stated with a smile.

Daphne was a weird one but cool. I smiled again as I crept into homeroom 111 and closed the door. As we watched the televised announcements, there was Nathan Simms giving out the news of the upcoming events. As I sat in my seat and listened to the announcements, Joshua

Salisbury made the effort to sit next to me. His brown eyes stared into mine, and he smiled.

"Hi."

That was it? That was all he said. I remember thinking that he wasn't much of a talker. I just smiled in return and listened more intently to the announcement.

"Good morning, Eagles," the television speakers blared out. "Here are the announcements for the day."

Chapter 5

It was later that Toby and I decided to take a drive to the lighthouse on Mount Desert Island. It was a half-hour drive down the coastline. I only hoped that the old Beetle would make it that far, for it had traveled a great distance already. Mom would kill me if it died now, not to mention the embarrassment of it happening in front of all the other kids. Besides, it was our only mode of transportation at the time. Toby remained quiet through the drive. He was upset at the fact that he wasn't the one in the driver's seat. To be cool, Toby took the convertible top down. I didn't like it very much. It was fall already, and I hated the cold. I laughed as I turned in my brother's direction. His face seemed to distort from the force of the wind as we drove faster. His cheeks flapped against the harsh current of air. He reminded me of a dog that poked his head out for fresh air. That act seemed to lift up his spirits. He reminded me of a kid in a candy aisle, trying to get a handful of the latest toffees. He turned to look at me and smiled. I couldn't help laughing at how he looked.

I cringed as I realized we were approaching a short bridge that connected the mainland to the island. I relaxed as we crossed. I couldn't believe that our fellow students traveled a half hour to go to a lighthouse, of all places. Didn't they hang at the mall like normal kids? I didn't understand until we approached it. The lighthouse stood in silent repose. The building towered over the bluffs of the Atlantic Ocean. The blue water and the rustic terrain gave the scenery its own charm. We pulled over to the side of the road and walked the rest of the distance. The wind was soft and the sunlight felt good as it warmed my bones. I could only hope that I would soon get used to this weather. A few tall pine trees were a lush green surrounded the lighthouse. It was like a blanket securing the structure from the harsh salts of the sea. I cupped my forehead with my hands like a visor to see it more clearly.

It was a white building with red trim. The beacon that signaled the sailors at sea was encased in glass and embraced in a red steel enclosure. I thought I saw a silhouette of someone standing on the balcony. I pulled out my phone and took pictures of the brick building. When I moved the phone down from my view, the person was no longer there.

"I have to show this to Mom. She loves this stuff," I said excitedly.

Toby gave a slight cough and uttered something, but I couldn't hear. He then said, "Are you sure that it's Mom we're talking about or you?" I smacked his arm and he laughed at me. "You girls are so hopelessly lost in your fantasy worlds. Life isn't a fairy tale, Amanda."

I begged to differ. "Who says it can't be?"

He smirked. "Me!"

"Well," I began, "that's your opinion. Hold still while I take a picture."

Toby posed with that smirk still on his face. I hated that cocky grin, but that was Toby. I wouldn't have him any other way. As Toby moved away, I looked down at the picture and frowned. The image was distorted. With a slight sigh, I just deleted the picture reluctantly and decided that I would take another picture later. I looked farther in the distance and could see a crowd of people around a bonfire by the water's edge. We walked over to it.

"Hey, guys, look who decided to show up. It's the girl from Cali," Joshua stated.

I waved like the queen of England and walked closer. That's when I could hear the topic of conversation.

"Did you hear what happened to Nathan?" one of the boys asked.

"Hear or see?" another asked.

I closed my eyes briefly and looked at Toby in silent warning.

Joshua took over conversation. "You mean his slight slip."

The crowd laughed hard.

"Slip of what?" I asked.

"Come on, Amanda, you saw it yourself," Josh stated impatiently.

A girl in the crowd said, "Someone put a whoopee cushion on Nathan's seat. When he sat down, it sounded like he broke wind on camera."

"Oh, come on, Cheryl. You can say fart," Joshua suggested with a laugh. He looked at me with a twinkle in his eye. "Come on, guys," Josh stated. "He can be fun to hang with sometimes, but other times the guy is a pain. Besides, that's not what happened. Nathan had a bad case of the runs. I heard from someone that he crapped himself in the hallway."

I looked at Toby again but said nothing.

Joshua looked up as he was taking a drink of tea out of a bottle. Wiping his mouth with his sleeve, he greeted us with a big "Hi."

Toby didn't respond, so I said "Hi" for the both of us.

"Nathan isn't coming here, is he?" I asked with trepidation. I didn't want Toby in another fight.

"No, he's not," another said. "I'm Jack."

"Hi."

Jack asked, "What brings you here?" with an outstretched arm.

"Daphne mentioned it to me today."

I heard the others make a noise. It sounded like pain. Cheryl started, "You mean Daphne Shikoba? You've got to be joking. She's strange."

I was starting not to like this girl. "Really?" I crossed my arms in defiance. "How so?"

Cheryl hesitated before talking and then started in a bit of a stutter. "All she does is waste her life at a library. She dresses in black, and at times I swear she talks in tongues. She's as weird as——"

"Really," I interrupted her, "as weird as the girl that lives in the house on the hill on Water Street?"

Toby stood by me steadfastly. He knew that I was unhappy. Daphne was the only person besides Joshua who was nice to me. I wasn't going to let this girl talk about her like that.

"No, that's not what I mean. You didn't have a choice where to live. Daphne has a choice on how she should dress."

That was it.

"Okay." Toby grabbed my arm. "Time to go, it's getting late."

As we started to walk back to the lighthouse, Jack caught our attention.

"What's the rush?" Jack asked. "Don't leave too soon. You'll miss the show."

I couldn't help asking, "What show?"

"Marcus. I heard he's back."

Joshua looked surprised. "You're kidding me."

Jack shook his head side to side. "Marcus always comes out before sunset to West Point. The locals call him a bad seed, but he can be cool. I told him that we would be here today. He doesn't talk much, but man, he's a blast."

I was flabbergasted. "A blast?"

"You'll see if you stick around," Amber responded as she looked at my brother and me. That's all my brother needed was a silent invitation from a girl to stay. What a sucker.

Joshua didn't look happy at all. "I thought he was still in juvy from busting up Nathan's car."

"I like him already," Toby whispered in my ear.

Jake said with his arms outstretched, "He's out now. Besides he's eighteen. He's an adult now."

Cheryl shook her head. "An adult with no future or education."

"That's not entirely true," Jack spoke out. "I heard he got his GED when he was locked up."

Cheryl just exhaled loudly in frustration.

I moved over to Jack. "What's with her?"

Jack smiled. "Cheryl and Marcus were a thing at one time. Marcus dumped her."

"He did NOT!" Cheryl screamed loudly.

"Yeah." He laughed, knowing full well he was pushing her buttons. "He did."

Cheryl came over and punched Jack in the gut. He twisted her around and hugged her close. "You got the better end of the deal. You've got me now."

Cheryl giggled as Jack squeezed tighter. Then he looked up at Toby and me. "Marcus is in a league of his own."

Joshua stared at Jack in astonishment. "You sound like

you actually like him."

Jack just shrugged. "You and he were best friends at one time, Josh. You have no room to talk."

That was when we heard the sound. I couldn't make out what it was at first. The closer it came, the more defined it was. The old Harley drove up the path to the bonfire quickly. It stopped a short distance from us. The rider took off his helmet and put it on the seat behind him. The tide increased and the sky above began to rumble. As I experienced the events, I couldn't help thinking of *pathetic fallacy*, a term used when we believe that nature and objects are human and have their own personality. The drastic change in the environment was like a bad omen. It was nature's way of saying trouble was coming. It reminded me of one of those movies when you know something surprising was about to happen. He turned off the motor and dropped the kickstand down on the bike. I saw the rider rub his fingers through his short, black hair.

My attention was deferred briefly as I heard the cheering and shouting of the others behind me. When I looked back I noticed that he wore a black shirt and it was torn slightly in the front. His jeans were about in the same condition. He walked forward with determination and confidence. I felt intimidated by his presence, but I didn't show it. I just shook it off, thinking that I was just overwhelmed with the whole situation of moving and being in a new environment. He was tall, maybe five feet, nine inches, with a tanned complexion. The thing that was the most interesting about him was his eyes. They were a dark shade of blue. They were almost like the color of violet. He smiled at everyone, showing a perfect pair of white teeth.

Joshua was the first to say something. "I thought they locked you up and threw away the key, Marcus."

Marcus's features changed when Joshua spoke, and he stared intensely at him. "Not likely."

"Just got out?" another asked.

Marcus turned his sights back on me. "I've been out for about a week or two."

I felt uneasy, like the guy was assessing me.

It was Jack's turn to speak. "Why haven't you been out at West Point till now?"

Still staring at me, he said, "I didn't have a reason to."

The teens laughed and cheered.

"You doin' the jump tonight or what?" Josh asked.

"What?" was the only word that escaped my lips.

Joshua walked closer to Marcus and slapped him on the back. "Our buddy Marcus here likes to feel a rush. He jumps the cliffs by the lighthouse with his bike."

The blood drained from my face. This was completely crazy and childish. A person must really have a death wish to do an act such as that. Josh pointed over to the gorge far in the distance. The deep ravine gave its silent welcome to all that dared. The length between the void was filled with fog. It would seem from this view that it would indeed have a deep ravine. Who was this guy, a stunt devil? The sound of Marcus's voice brought me back to the present.

"Not today," Marcus stated, "I don't jump anymore."

"Since when?" Cheryl asked out of curiosity.

Another voice emanated from the crowd. "Come on, Marcus, you're the man."

Marcus shouted, "Actually, I only came out 'cause Daphne asked me to make sure her friend Amanda was all right."

Cheryl scoffed and snorted. "You can tell Daphne Mandy is fine."

I turned and corrected her. "It's Amanda."

Marcus smiled at me and then coughed out loud before a laugh escaped him. "Well, at least I know now Amanda is fine." He dipped his head closer to me and whispered, "This is not the crowd for you."

I crossed my arms. "How would you know what my type of crowd was?" I crossed my arms defiantly. "And how did you know who I was?"

Marcus smiled again. "Small town," he answered with an outstretched hand, "and yours is the only new face I see."

I wasn't sure, but I thought I heard someone make the sound of a cat hissing. I pinched Toby hard on the arm for some assistance.

Toby then spoke out to ease the tension surrounding

us. "She's fine, thanks. We were just leaving. I have to get the car back soon."

Marcus still stared at me, not budging a bit.

"I am fine, thanks," I stated in an angry tone. I felt that I was being manhandled in a way.

Marcus seemed to hesitate at first. He stared at me as if he was puzzled by something. The intensity of his stare unnerved me. His forehead furrowed slightly, then just as quickly, he spoke out. "Okay, then. My job's done here."

Marcus looked as though he was angry. Toby held his hand out to Marcus, but he didn't take it. Marcus wasn't moving. It was as though he was waiting for us to go before he took his own leave.

"All right then." Toby could feel the animosity and sudden resentment that came from Marcus. Toby smiled in a knowing way and took me by the arm. "Say good-bye, Mandy."

I stared at Toby in horror; talk about sibling rivalry. I knew my brother liked to ruffle my feathers, but that took the cake. I decided to not say a word and deal with him later. "Bye, everybody, I'll see you in school."

Marcus stood still in front of us. I don't know what I did to this guy, but something bothered him. His frown changed into a smile. "So welcome to Maine, Mandy." The sarcasm seeped through his lips.

"Yes," I stated, "the frigid temperatures are truly delightful. Are you my welcoming committee?" I couldn't wait to get away from this guy.

Marcus shut his eyes briefly from the blow of words that hit his pride. I thought I saw a slight flinch as well. My words seemed to affect him. Maybe he wasn't used to it.

He didn't waste time to respond, "Well, try to enjoy your stay, no matter how short it may be."

I was confused; how was this conversation turned on me? A bit of fun on Marcus's part was turning into a dispute, and I didn't even know him. I figured that Daphne told him about where we lived. I rubbed my face in a circular motion. "Look," I stated with a sigh of frustration, "tell Daphne I appreciate her concern." When I looked up at his face, his expression changed to a softer look. "Thanks for coming out, but I am fine."

"Yeah, it's all cool," Toby said behind me.

I didn't even realize that my brother wasn't next to me anymore. I looked over my shoulder at him and gave him a look that he knew well. I thought my brother was being a coward. Marcus seemed a bit surprised by the sudden thank you and moved aside so Toby and I could walk past him. He gave a slight bow and raised his left hand as if gesturing us to walk in that direction.

"Come on, Marcus," someone shouted out, "jump."

Cheryl even tried to egg Marcus on as well, but she saw that his thoughts and eyes were preoccupied with the girl leaving the bonfire. "Marcus," she shouted, making him turn in her direction. "Are you jumping or what?"

Marcus gave Cheryl a look of disgust. "No."

The teens were awing in disappointment.

Marcus turned looked back to where he was going. "It's called growing up, guys. See ya around." Marcus got on the bike and turned on the motor.

As Toby and I started the car, we saw Marcus fly right past us.

Chapter 6

As I was driving home, I was irritated with Marcus. I mean, I didn't even know the guy. Then again, knowing Daphne, she probably continuously nagged the guy to come see me. I wondered how she knew Marcus. I figured I would ask her when I saw her in school. I eased back into my seat. The tension was slowly draining from me as I looked out into the sea. Daphne was right. I did love the change of scenery, but it was only because it reminded me of home. I could hear the seagulls. That put a smile on my face. I think Daphne knew that this was what I needed. She was very perceptive and a good judge of character. I didn't care what the others said; I liked the girl, and nothing would change that. I inhaled deeply and became lost to my inner thoughts. Marcus was cute, even though he was a pushy person. I smiled to myself. He seemed shocked when I was defiant. I think that he wasn't used to that kind of treatment.

I was glad that the top of the Beetle was back up. The sun was down and the night air was cold. I shivered and moved over to the heater to turn it on full blast. Toby grinned.

"Better," I said out loud.

"Don't worry, sis, we'll get used to the climate change."

I stared out into the darkness, watching the moonlight rays touch the ocean's surface. I scooted farther into the vinyl seat and contemplated. "Toby?"

"Yes."

I hesitated before I asked the question at hand. "Do you ever think of Dad?"

"Of course I do."

I waited a few seconds more. "Do you, do you ever dream about him?"

Toby shrugged. "I don't know. Maybe, sometimes. Why?"

"Do you ever ask Mom about him?"

"All right. Amanda, where is this conversation going?" he asked with impatience as he briefly looked at me.

I moved deeper into the seat. "Nothing. Never mind. Forget I asked." I changed the subject. "I saw that Amber girl was looking at you."

He took the bait. "And I happened to notice that Marcus took quite an interest in you," he stated as fact.

"You've gotta be joking," I said defiantly. "The guy is trouble. You heard Joshua."

"Well, if you ask me, Joshua didn't like the competition. That was abundantly clear."

"Wow, Toby has a larger vocabulary than I thought." I laughed. "Do you know what *abundantly* means?"

"Yes. Do you know what *shut up* means?"

"Okay, okay. No need to get sensitive."

"You wouldn't know what *sensitive* meant even if it came up and slapped you."

I slapped his arm playfully. "Funny. Very funny. So what did you do to Nathan?"

Toby just looked in my direction and smiled. When I turned back to the road, that's when I shouted at a shadow. I slammed on the brakes. As the thick fog began to separate, the shadow became clear. The car skidded to a halt right in front of the beast. It stood its ground, unmoving. The animal was brilliant. Light shades of brown highlighted its eyes. He was old and had seen many battles. One of his antlers was broken, but it gave the animal character. It stood silent, giving out its curious stare. I could feel the ground beneath me rumble as the creature stomped its hooves.

Toby's breathing was just as hard as my own. "You stupid animal."

I grabbed Toby's arm in warning. "Don't excite him."

"Excite him? Excite him? What about me?"

"Do you want him to charge the car? Just wait."

The breathing of the animal was steady and slow. The mist that formed from its nose dissipated as fast as it began. Its breath rose upward, into the night, until it was no longer seen. Its eyes looked out at us briefly again, and he gave a slight nod of its head. I was still trying to catch my breath. The great old beast gazed at us as if asking a silent question. It wasn't skittish or angered. It just stared, mesmerized by the light of the car. It slowly started to move toward us and then stopped, raising its ears, looking in the darkness. With great reluctance, it moved backwards and then slowly walked back into the brush. It took me a minute to find my voice. "Did you know Maine had moose?" I finally asked as I began to breathe again.

Toby looked at me as if I were crazy. "Does it look like I knew that Maine had moose?"

I rolled my eyes as I continued to drive home. Toby seemed salty as ever.

"It was gorgeous," I said in wonder.

"It wouldn't have been if we hit it." It took Toby a few moments to regain his composure.

I gave him a disgusted look. "I have never seen one so up close before."

Toby decided that he wanted to be dropped off in front of the local drugstore when he saw some friends from school. The rain started when I hit Water Street. When I arrived home, all was quiet. I was happy to see a completed roof. I had no worries about getting drenched this evening. I regretted my decision of not staying with Toby the minute I closed the front door of the house. The only sound that emanated throughout this prison was the distant pattering of the rain. I jumped up when I heard a noise and then held my hand to my heart, hoping to regain a sense of calm. That was the one thing I hated about houses, especially old ones. When the wood expands and contracts, it makes loud popping noises. I still didn't remove myself from the foyer. I peered into the darkness looking for the light switch. I couldn't find it.

I ran my hands across the wall in hopes of finding it on the second try. I felt the light brush of a gust of wind across my back. My first thought was that it was just an old, drafty house. I didn't want my thoughts to move in any other direction. I didn't want to scare myself. The pattering of the rain increased to a sound like flood waters outside. I smiled in victory when I found the switch. The light turned on with a slight humming noise as the chandelier above me flickered on and off. "Figures," I said out loud, "now the wiring needs fixing."

I tried to brush myself off as best I could. It was an attempt to avoid making puddles of water on the floor below me. Mom had put in ceramic tile. She did it herself and was proud of it. I didn't want to ruin her tile job. As I grazed my hands across my clothing, some beads of water dripped onto the mat Mom left out at the base of the door. I laughed out loud at the irony of it all. I knew I would still get some water on the floor. I removed my shoes and walked over to the small closet to place them inside. I then went to the study to look for a good book to read while Mom and Toby were away.

I jumped again when I heard the crack of lightning. It was so loud it sounded like a whip. Fall in Maine was a dreary one. I heard that the highest temperatures in summer were in the sixties. I tried to erase that thought as I got closer to the study door. When I opened it, I thought it was strange that the light was left on. I could hear the wind pressure on the window next to me. The stained glass was vibrant with color after all its years. The background was in emerald green and the picture was that of a vase filled with roses. Every window in that room had the same depiction. I scolded myself for not noticing it before. I was usually observant when it came to detail. The bright light from the storm blazed through the window into my eyes.

I went to the book shelves and rummaged and scanned the binders of the books until I found something of interest. I saw one called one called *The Bastille*. Sounded like a good read. I liked the way the word rolled off the tongue. It was a weird thing, titles. They can grab a reader just from a single word. I began to open the book and then I dropped it when I heard a sound. I stood still and silent in hopes to hear Mom's or Toby's voice. When I didn't hear anything else, I bent down to pick up the book. I scolded myself thinking that I was still a bit rattled from the moose event in the car. When I grabbed the novel from its resting place, the sound came yet again. It was a loud banging noise that emanated from a distant room. It sounded as if it came from the kitchen, but I couldn't be sure. I thought I heard a whisper afterwards and then a cough.

I slowly walked in the direction of the sound, keeping

to the shadows so I wasn't seen. When I arrived at the family room, I saw a poker and ash pan on the stand next to the fireplace. Trying to keep my wits about myself, I picked them both up so I had one for each hand. My palms were sweating and my heart was pounding in my throat. I could actually hear my heart beating in my ears. My trepidation escalated into a state of pure panic. I couldn't stop shaking. It was an old house. I kept telling myself *you're letting your imagination run wild,* yet I was afraid to shout out and say something. The light from the storm illuminated the kitchen door, casting a bright white contrast along its seams.

I hated the storm outside; it made the situation worse. The loud sound of the violent weather was drowning out whatever noise was coming from the kitchen. Maybe it was a burglar. As I gazed at the kitchen door, I stood, waiting for something, but what? I didn't see any shadows under the closed entryway. It was silent again. I held my breath before I opened the door that separated me from the room. The lightning flashed and revealed nothing but an empty kitchen with an opened window above the sink. The window continuously rattled in the window sill. I walked over to close the glass window that caused all my dread. The window continued its violent rapping against its frame as the rain water forced its entry into the home in a wild downpour. The droplets hit my skin sharply, causing a slight sting to my bare arms. I placed the poker down and reached outward, holding the window and pulling.

I locked the latch and stared briefly outward into the storm. I placed my open palms on the cold granite countertop, feeling its texture. The brightness of the lightning distorted my vision. The bright colors of yellow and green slowly died down as my sight returned. I made a quick check to make sure that the window was locked. When I was satisfied with my work, I turned quickly to leave the room. That's when it happened.

There it was, shaking in the shadows. I wasn't sure what it was at first. I thought it was Taboo, that she was in the kitchen, and then I thought it was just a silhouette that was cast by the activities of the storm outside. I crouched down and narrowed my eyes to focus on the eerie form. The jittering continued, and it began to move. I jumped backwards, hitting my back on the counter behind me. It looked as if it was trying to catch its breath. I jumped again when I heard it cry out suddenly. I covered my ears from the screeching. Was it a wild animal that had wandered in from the window? Judging from its size, it wasn't an animal. I couldn't scream. I couldn't do anything. I was paralyzed with complete fright.

I could hear what sounded like cracking bones as the figure moved its head. It raised its hand from the shadows. As it did this motion, the sounds of its tendons made a sharp, ear-piercing snap, like the sound of splitting wood. The form was horrid and the noises it made were horrible.

It slowly scooted forward, toward me. My feet were planted on the floor. Time seemed to slow down with the movements of the unknown specter. I held the ash pan in one hand and reached out behind me for the poker that I placed on the counter. My breathing was shallow. I didn't want to take my eyes off the stranger. If this was a dream, I wanted to wake up. The storm was drowning out the sounds the sinister form made as it moved toward me. I could hear the wheezing as it tried to take a breath.

I whimpered out loud as I reached out but couldn't feel the poker. The lightning enhanced the illumination in the room and gave me a brief, clear image of the specter. I finally screamed, releasing my inner fears. It was a man, or at least it looked like a man. One of his legs was broken. As he moved closer, I could hear the unpleasant sound of the leg being dragged across the floor. I continued reaching outward, in hopes of feeling the coldness of metal on my hands. My thoughts wandered franticly, trying to readjust myself to the situation. I stopped feeling for the poker when I heard the sound of it being dragged against the floor. The intruder curled it hands around the poker and used it to brace itself to walk. The specter coughed and gagged, and something spilled from its mouth. Sticky blood flowed onto the floor from its lips. I regained my wits and tried to run, but I stopped at the door when I heard it speak. It didn't sound human.

"Please, help me."

The plea was so soft I could barely hear the words. It didn't matter what was said. The terror was so great within me that my instincts took over. I continued to move toward the kitchen door in hopes of an escape. I grabbed the latch on the door, but it wouldn't open. I pulled and pulled, but it was no use. The sound was too close for comfort. I kicked the door and screamed. I was afraid to turn around.

"Please." The voice almost sounded childlike.

I felt a slight touch on my back. I turned, pushing on the door. His face was ashen, and his body convulsed. The liquid spewed again from him as he tried to speak. I could hear the gurgling sound coming from his mouth. He grabbed the front of my shirt.

"Please don't hurt me," I screamed as I fought.

He coughed, and fluid spilled on my shirt as the creature held it in a tight grip. I screamed loudly as I tried to break free. As I moved aside, I felt the fabric on my shirt tear. I could hear the poker slide as the creature attempted to hold its weight against it. The poker gave way, refusing to take the added pressure. The creature's balance shifted with the loss of the poker. It lost its grip on my shirt, leaving it without leverage. The heavy metal made a loud clang as it fell to the floor taking the intruder with it. I ran to the back door of the kitchen, fumbling with the lock in hopes of escape.

I could hear the poker being dragged again as he moved

in my direction. I couldn't look behind me. I tried to put all my concentration on the task at hand. I pressed my weight on the door, and it broke free. Adrenaline coursed through my veins as I bolted from the home. I turned toward the opened door to see if he gave chase. He was gone. The room looked empty. I rubbed my eyes, trying to make sense of it all. I didn't want to go back in the house. I wasn't going to take the chance. In a state of panic, I ran two miles down the road in search of help. A local family pulled over when I flagged them down. I called my mother to deter her from going to the house. My mother in turn called the police.

We didn't go back home that night. My mother thought it would be safer for us to check into the hotel in the center of town. The police went out and checked the scene to make sure the man was gone. I tried to make sense of what had happened to me. Was it right for me not to tell them everything that I saw? They would not have believed me if I told them the entire story. Mom thought maybe the man was hurt and startled me, looking for help. The house was very secluded from other residences. I agreed with Mom, the more I thought on it. She thought maybe he had gotten into an accident after I described to her what he looked like.

The police took down my description of the suspect and left. I sat on the bed in the hotel room, not speaking. I was still terrified. His bloodshot eyes had seemed distant, as if he were in a crazed state. The eyes were cold and disheartening. Was he just as terrified as me? Was he in a complete state of panic and pain? As I played the scene back in my mind, it seemed unreal. Instances such as these happen only in horror films, they didn't happen to real people. I became disgusted with myself, but he terrified me. Why would a person break into someone's house if his intent was not to hurt or steal? Maybe Mom was right. I cupped my hands in my face. The blood, there was so much of it. I did hear banging. Maybe he thought no one was home. I rubbed my hands together, hoping to get warm within.

I was so deep in my thoughts that I didn't notice that my mother sat bedside me, waiting for me to speak. All that awaited her was a cry that started deep within me and escaped from my lips. My mother held me, hoping to calm my fears. She tried, but it didn't comfort me. I questioned my own sanity as I looked around the small hotel room. If this man was hurt, were did he go? It was as if he disappeared into the walls. I know what I saw, but the blood, the blood was gone from my clothes. All that remained on the fabric was mud and rain water.

I continued to hold my mother tightly, hoping for inner calm. Toby just rubbed my shoulders from behind me. I thought I heard him curse, but I wasn't sure. Toby hurt when I hurt, but being a boy, he had his own way of expressing anger and fear. I didn't want to go back to that house, but I knew that eventually I would have to.

The police returned to the room, and they confirmed my fears. The man was gone without a trace. They had found the poker on the kitchen floor. They had indicated to Mom that they would take it and dust for prints. They also stated that the house was secure. Mom disagreed. We stayed at the hotel, for that night, anyway.

Chapter 7

I sat in class on Thursday morning in a daze. I hadn't been to school for a few days, but Mom thought it was for the best. We were home now and all was as quiet as before. The locals knew of the events that had occurred that night. In this small town everybody knew everything. Later we found that there had been no accidents on the roads that evening. The only other assumption was that the man had been a hunter and was injured in the woods, but there were no hospitals in or around town that had treated any patients with the injuries that I had described. There were so many wounds that were on the man. Did I imagine it, or was I going crazy?

I decided to go to Daphne's house after class. Mom thought it was a good idea to be with a friend. Daphne had called me after I spent two days of not being in school. She was a good person and listened to what I had to say. I hadn't seen her for almost a week. I was missing her, and getting out of that house would do me some good. She had told me before school that her brother was going to pick us up. I didn't know that she had a brother. She had never mentioned him before.

When school ended, I walked outside to find Daphne

waiting for me with smiles at the front of the Ellsworth High School's main doors. She was at the bottom of the steps, standing on one of the pedestal caps, waving her arms at me. I laughed and then tried to cover my mouth so she didn't see. She jumped from the brick structure and walked quickly in my direction.

"I should have told you before to hurry," she said as she adjusted her book bag on her shoulder. "My brother doesn't like to be kept waiting, and he isn't allowed on school grounds."

Daphne grabbed my hand forcefully and submerged us into the crowd, looking for her brother's car. I couldn't help giggling at her distressed facial expression.

"Daphne, it's okay. What does your brother's car look like?"

"It's not my brother's car. It's my father's," she stated with impatience. "It's a Jaguar."

"Well, your dad has good taste."

"Well, it's not like he can't afford it. He's a lawyer."

I arched my brow at her. "Really? Lucky you."

She stared at me with a tad bit of resentment. "It has its rewards and downfalls. Especially if your father is so entangled in his work he doesn't have time for you."

"I am sorry, Daphne." I didn't know what to say. I was at a loss for words. "I didn't mean—"

"Yeah," she said interrupting me. "I know."

"What color is it?" I asked, changing the subject.

"The only color that looks best on a Jag. Black."

I laughed again. "Okay."

She stopped momentarily when she spotted the car. "Come on, he's going to kill me."

I continued to laugh as we approached the car. I stopped laughing when she opened the door. I looked at her as I crossed my arms. "Your brother?"

I couldn't believe it. Sitting on the driver's side was none other than Marcus, so the pieces fit. I'd had better days than this. Daphne got in the back seat and shut the door. "Don't just stand there. Get in before the principal sees us," Daphne screamed in a panic.

"What?" I was speechless.

"You know. Nathan. Car. Expulsion. Marcus isn't allowed on the grounds. Get in."

Marcus crossed his own arms as he watched me and relished my embarrassment. His couldn't conceal his wicked grin. He removed his sunglasses from his face. "It's okay, Daph." Marcus opened the passenger door. "You heard the boss, Amanda." He smiled in triumph. "Get in."

I had no choice but to get in and drive away with Marcus Shikoba, the so-called bad boy. As Marcus put the car in drive, Joshua called out to him. Marcus waited for Joshua to walk over. Joshua then placed his palms on the vehicle. Marcus put his glasses on his face and turned his face in Joshua's direction. I also happened to notice that Marcus was gripping the steering wheel in a tight manner.

SHADOWS

It would appear that there was bad blood between the two.

"Hey, rich boy." Joshua didn't seem as nice to Marcus as he had the night before.

Marcus didn't take the bait. Instead he smiled back. "What do you want, Josh?"

"I think it's obvious."

"Okay," Daphne chimed in. "That's enough. Let's go home, Mark."

Daphne must have known something that I didn't.

"Yeah, Mark, why don't you go home?"

Marcus revved the engine of the Jag a bit. I could feel the tension escalate between the two rivals.

Joshua looked in my direction. "Amanda, do you need a ride?"

Marcus dropped his glasses down a bit and eyed Joshua like a predator. "I think she has one already," he stated with an air of finality and smiled.

Joshua grabbed Marcus's shoulder in a silent warning. Marcus placed the gear back in Park and began to open the door. I didn't know what to do. I didn't understand what this macho scene was all about. Before Marcus could get out of the car, I grabbed his arm and tugged him in my direction. "It's all right."

Marcus stared at me, confused, as I looked out to Joshua. "I asked him to pick us up, Josh. Everything's fine. I didn't know that it would create a problem." Marcus stared at me knowing of the lie.

Josh's features changed into an expression of defeat. "Well, now you know."

I had never seen Joshua ever act like that. I didn't like it. Marcus pushed his sunglasses back up the bridge of his nose and smiled in victory. "She learns quickly, doesn't she, Josh?"

Joshua's face turned bright red in anger as Marcus moved the car with Joshua's hands still on the door frame. It was good timing as well. The principal had heard of Marcus's arrival and was walking out of the main entryway of the school to talk to him.

As the car passed the gates of the school, Marcus briefly turned in my direction and then looked back to the road. "I wouldn't hang with Joshua Salisbury. He's trouble."

"Funny," I said with my arms still crossed. "I hear the same about you." I smiled back sheepishly.

He dropped his sunglasses to look at me. "I may be trouble. That much is true. But there is a difference between him and me. My kind of trouble is the fun kind."

I couldn't help it. I had to laugh. It was funny. Daphne remained quiet. Marcus actually wasn't such a bad character. I talked about California and how I ended up living on Water Street. He listened but didn't say much.

"So what is a name like Shikoba? Is it Italian? French?"

"Nope," Daphne finally said. "It's from the nation of Choctaw. Our mother was Irish, but our father is Wabinaki and Choctaw."

I stared at her, confused.

"Native American," Marcus chimed in.

"Nice," I stated interested, "I myself am a Heinz 57 variety."

It was Daphne's turn to laugh. "Meaning?"

I smiled in returned, "Oh, you know, as far as heritage. I probably have a little bit of everything. To be honest, my Mom doesn't tell me much. I couldn't tell you anything about my family history." I smiled.

Daphne had a twinkle in her eye. "A name can tell a lot about a person, so they say. If you're ever interested, we can look through family trees and trace your roots back."

"And how would you do that?"

"Easy," she stated with vigor. "It's called the Internet. Ever heard of it?" Daphne's mannerism changed. "I heard about what happened at your house. Are you okay?"

I smiled weakly. "Yeah, sure. Tough as nails. I was a bit shook up, but I am better."

Daphne placed her hand on my shoulder for comfort. "I am glad."

I laughed a bit. "You sound just like my mother. So what does Shikoba mean?" I asked, changing the subject back to heritage.

Daphne smiled wider. "Feather."

I was surprised to find that Daphne lived on Mount Desert Island. I turned in her direction as we crossed the small bridge that connected the island to the main coast.

She shrugged. "Our dad owns a lot of properties on this island, including the lighthouse by the cliffs. It's been in the family for generations. My grandfather encouraged my father to go to law school. As he put it, 'The white man's word holds no truth.'" She looked back at me. "He wanted my dad to make sure that all lands that belonged to our nation stayed that way. The contracts and papers, along with the deeds were drawn up. Developers are always trying to buy from us, but Father and Grandfather say it's our people's land not ours. Grandfather always tries to preserve the old ways. He doesn't want us to forget who we are or where we came from. Family, lineage, and truth; this is the way of our people."

Marcus looked in the rearview mirror. "You sound more like that man every day."

"Thanks," was her only response.

It was nice that no one mentioned the events of last week. It would have made things awkward, for I couldn't explain them myself. I only hoped that the man would be eventually found if he was hurt. I still questioned myself on the events of that night, and I was there. My thoughts turned back to the present. "Does your grandfather live with you?"

It was Marcus's turn to speak. "No, he doesn't like the way we live. Believe it or not, Grandfather lives on Water Street. He's in the home his grandfather built and doesn't want to leave. When you get set in your ways, there's no changing them."

I looked out into the sea. "I would like to meet him sometime."

"Sure," Marcus stated. "Just say when you want to go."

"How about now?" I stated, crossing my arms again.

Marcus smiled, turned the wheel, and went back in the direction we came.

I didn't realize how long Water Street was. We traveled the winding road, stopped by a dirt path, and turned onto it. At first I thought we took a wrong turn, but the cabin appeared in the wooded lot like magic. It was nice, shaded, and secluded. The rustic look of the home gave it some charm. The green trees swayed in welcome. It seemed peaceful. I could hear the sound of wood being chopped as I got out of the car. Marcus cupped his hand around his mouth to amplify his voice. "*Aki?*"

As his voice echoed in the distance, a small man dressed in jeans and a plaid shirt emerged from around the building. He looked very happy to see Marcus and Daphne. He waved back and yelled, "*Amafo*, Marcus." The old man laughed and shook his head from side to side.

I turned to Daphne, curious about what was said. "Marcus called him father. He is reminding Marcus that he is his grandfather. He raised us, so to Marcus, he is our father. I don't think he'll ever call him *Amafo*."

Daphne ran to the man with open arms and held him tightly.

"*Halito, chim Achukma*," Grandfather Shikoba said as he returned the embrace.

Daphne laughed. "Yes, grandfather. I am good."

I followed the Shikobas to the back of the house. Its appearance showed that it was definitely a place where a man lived. There was nothing feminine to it. There was no garden and no flowers. There were many wood carvings and what appeared to be dream catchers in the yard. When I walked over and touched one, Daphne chimed in, "They are medicine wheels. They help create balance of all energies." She pointed to the right of the wheel. "East, this represents change." She then pointed to the left of the sphere. "West, symbol of healing. North is where everything begins. South is passion and fire. Center is where all balance is created."

I jumped when I heard her grandfather's voice from behind me. "*Achukma*, Daphne. Very good."

Daphne's grandfather continued to stare at the medicine wheel. He held his hand out and gestured for me to hold it. I smiled and thanked him. Daphne repeated what I said in their language.

"His English is not very good," Marcus said as he stood on the porch.

"Better than yours," his grandfather responded.

Daphne looked at Grandfather stunned. He smiled and said, "Television. I can speak some English, but no want to. Come," he said as he held out his hand to me.

When I went to place the medicine wheel back in its resting spot, the elderly man held my hand steadfast. "*Haloka*, you keep. This is *aholloko*, sacred to my people."

"No, I can't."

The elderly man stared deep into my eyes. "*A*."

"Grandfather says 'yes.'" Marcus came from behind me and placed the leather lace around my neck. He then tied it to hold it in place. "When you get home, put this in your room. Hang it by your window. Aki says that these bring balance into homes." Marcus walked closer toward his grandfather and began to speak to him in the language that I didn't understand.

Marcus's grandfather then asked, "What nation are you, Amanda?"

I shook my head, not understanding the question.

Marcus started by saying, "He wants to know what kind of Native American you are."

Marcus's grandfather gave him a scornful look.

"Oh." I laughed out of nervousness. "None that I know of." After a brief pause, I continued with "Both of my parents are from the U.K."

When Grandfather nodded, Daphne called me inside. Marcus and his grandfather stayed outside. They weren't out there for long. It appeared that they were in deep discussion. Whatever his grandfather had said put Marcus in a foul mood.

I looked around at their grandfather's dwelling. The

natural wood of the logs was varnished in the color of cherry. I loved the smell of the wood. The sweet scent of timber soothed me. I always loved the aroma, especially when it was freshly cut. Its dark contrast created a calm, relaxing environment. I touched a timber that was lacquered and felt its smooth texture with my fingertips. It seemed that the very structure itself was built for enlightenment and contemplation.

When Marcus came inside, he watched me intensely but didn't say much. He had been so talkative before we arrived. I didn't understand what the change was about. It seemed that whatever Marcus's grandfather had to say, he didn't like it very much.

Daphne spoke, breaking the silence. "Grandfather is a tribal elder. He tries to stay with the old ways of our culture and teaches the younger generation about their origins. He is also our people's medicine man."

Daphne was like an encyclopedia. I stood in amazement as I looked around the room. One bookcase to the left was filled with rolled scrolls, of what, I didn't know. The cabin was small but had enough room for one person to live comfortably. Their grandfather gestured for me to sit down. It was a wonderful visit, but it seemed the longer I stayed, the more agitated Marcus became. When we left the home, Marcus stayed in the log cabin to talk to his grandfather more.

"Your grandfather is nice," I told Daphne.

Daphne sat in silence in the back of the vehicle.

I turned around from the passenger's seat to look at her. "Why are you so quiet?"

"It was something my grandfather said." She looked up at me, confused. "He called you *Haloka*. It means *loved one*. You are the first white person my grandfather has ever talked to and liked."

I smiled and said, "He is probably mellowing in his older years."

Daphne rubbed her hands together. "He never treated my mother that way. He hated my mother," Daphne replied as she stared out the window.

"Oh, I am sorry."

"Don't be," she stated in anger. "She left us. She was a drunk, anyways." She took in a large breath before she said, "You're the only person who knows that, besides family. Grandfather is always a good judge of character." Daphne looked up at me. "I would take his approval as a compliment. He asked Marcus to bring you back again sometime."

"Really?" I scooted around, kneeling on the car seat and rested my face on the backs of my hands. "What else did he say?" I asked as I gloated.

Daphne stared back down at her hands. "I can't tell you."

That statement got my attention. "Why?"

Daphne looked up. "You wouldn't believe me if I told you."

I looked at her stunned. Marcus had walked outside and approached the car. He sat down and started the motor. He then shook his head. "What did you do to him?" he questioned, looking at me.

I just shrugged.

Marcus still continued to shake his head as we left the residence. "Well, it seems he has a soft side for you, *Haloka*."

I stayed silent, and Daphne looked at her brother wide-eyed. "She knows what it means."

"And?"

Daphne stayed quiet.

Marcus continued to drive. Marcus couldn't stand the silence in the car any longer. "Do you want to go home, Amanda, or would you like to hang around with us?"

It was nice to be out with friends. I really didn't want to go home just yet. "I'll go with you guys."

"All right," Marcus said and continued driving.

Chapter 8

The day with Marcus and Daphne was fun. Daphne was a bit off, after seeing her grandfather, but came around later. My heart went out to her. Not only to lose your mother but to feel abandoned by the one you love the most is unbearable. I could sense her inner pain, but I felt if she wanted to talk about it more, she would have done so. Daphne decided to stay behind when Marcus drove me home. It was already 9:00, and I knew if I stayed any longer, Mom would have my head. It was a bit uncomfortable, at first, being alone with Marcus, but after a while, we started talking again.

As we drove in the darkness, I couldn't help asking about Joshua. I know it wasn't right to start a drilling session, but I couldn't help it. It was my nature to do so. When I mentioned his name, though, Marcus's temperament changed. He said only that at one time they were very good friends, that time changes people and puts them on a different course.

I liked Marcus's eyes, for his eyes really expressed his emotions. I had never seen such a color. When he smiled, it made them sparkle like he had a mischievous plan. I noticed he had a dimple only on the right side of his cheek.

The more I looked at him, the more appealing he became. No wonder Cheryl was so upset when Marcus was finished with her. The more you got to know him, the easier it was to like him. We talked about his new job at the salvage yard and his plans for the future.

When we arrived back at my house, he placed the car in Park and turned in my direction. "Well, I hope you had fun today."

"Yes, I did. Thanks. I really needed it."

I reached over and gave him a hug of thanks, and he hugged me back.

"Are you sure you're okay?"

"Yes," I responded, knowing that he was talking about my ordeal with an intruder in the house.

When I turned and went to open the door, he called my name. "Aki asked me to give you something before you left today."

I held the medicine wheel and clutched it in my grasp. "Yes, tell him I said thanks again."

"No," he said, smiling. "He wanted me to give you something else. Now remember he asked me to give this to you, so if there is any complaint, you'll have to take it up with him, but you have to close your eyes."

I gave him a curious look and shook my head.

"You don't trust him?"

"I don't know your grandfather," I corrected him. He sat deeper in his seat. "Well, what about me?"

After a moment of hesitation, I said, "I don't really know you either."

Marcus arched his brow at me.

"All right. All right, I'll close my eyes." I laughed uncontrollably from embarrassment.

I held my hands out, but nothing was placed in them. I laughed again, waiting. That's when it happened. I felt Marcus's hand touching my face.

"What are you doing?"

Before I could open my eyes, Marcus Shikoba kissed me. I had never kissed a boy before. At first I was nervous. I could feel the brushing of his lips across mine in a seductive fashion. The kiss wasn't quick; it lingered. I had an intake of breath as he deepened the kiss. I wasn't an expert; I think he could tell. It wasn't what I expected. There was an explosion of emotions within me. I kissed him back and ran my fingers through his dark hair. I was surprised and afraid, all at the same time. Was it wrong to let him steal a kiss? It felt right. How did we both go from disliking each other to this? I never thought a kiss could be so powerful and wonderful. I wanted it to last, but he moved back. When I finally opened my eyes, he smiled, satisfied with himself.

"What was that about?"

"It's whatever you want it to be, Amanda." He placed his hand on my shoulder.

"Aki told me if I didn't kiss you, I would regret it."

I didn't know how to respond. I was at a loss for words. Should I be angry? It was just a kiss, after all. When I looked at the front of the house, I saw the light on the porch go on, so I went to grab the door handle of the car to leave. The deadly silence was awkward.

"I would like to see you again, Amanda," Marcus said from behind.

I turned in Marcus's direction. "You don't know much about me."

He grinned again. "I'd like to."

I bent over and picked up my book bag. "All right," I answered, licking my bottom lip slightly.

"What about we go and hang out at the lighthouse this weekend? There is something Aki wants me to show you. He said you would appreciate it."

"Sounds delightful," I responded with a smile back.

Without saying another word, I opened the car door and stepped outside. I saw my mother opening the door and looking at her watch. I turned out into the darkness and waved as Marcus turned around and left. I watched his taillights fade away and then walked to the front door.

Mom's face was in a scowl. "Amanda, it's after nine o'clock."

"I know, Mom. I'm sorry. I lost track of time." I walked past her, trying to walk away from the line of fire.

When we were both inside, Mom slammed the door shut. She was wearing her favorite beige sweater that tied in the front. Her hair was all bound up in a clip and she was wearing my fuzzy Taz slippers that she bought me for Christmas last year. I also noticed some blue paint that was smeared on her right cheek. I could tell she was on a painting kick. I wonder what creation was waiting for me upstairs. When Mom did her painting, it was always messy. She stood there waiting for an excuse from my lips for my absence, but none came. The silence between us was disturbing.

She started first. "Who's the boy, Amanda?"

"Marcus, Daphne's brother," I responded quickly. I turned toward the new stairs and began to walk up them in hopes of sneaking away.

"Amanda Marie, I am not done with you."

There it was. My middle name. That was when I knew I was in trouble. I stopped mid-stride, gripping the banister, praying for a miracle.

"I said it's after nine o'clock, young lady."

I pivoted in her direction, making a face.

"If I were you, I wouldn't roll your eyes at me, if you want to sleep easy tonight," she assured me, arching her brow.

"I am sorry, Mom. It won't happen again. I swear I lost track of time. I am only twenty minutes late."

"You should have called."

"Yes." What else could I say? If I didn't want to be grounded, I better just agree.

"Maybe a weekend indoors will jog your memory, lady."

"I am sorry, Mom. I know you were worried with all that has happened. I left my phone at home," I knowing lied. "When I realized the time, I couldn't call you in the car."

My mom eyed me up and down, contemplating my punishment. When she smiled, that's when I knew things were getting slowly worse. I was worried.

"Tomorrow you are going to help me in the basement. Then we are going to clean out the carriage house for the car, as well."

When my lips began to move, she held her hand up to silence me. She then placed her hands on her temples and moved them in a circular motion. I could tell that her head was aching. "All right, then," she said, placing her hands on her hips. "Now I'm done with you. I hope your day out was worth it." By the smile that displayed on my face, she knew I thought so.

I ran upstairs into the hallway. It was nice not taking a detour into the kitchen to gain access upstairs. I didn't go in there much since the incident. If I did, I wasn't alone. Mom had changed all the locks on the doors and installed dead bolts to ensure our safety. When I went into my room, I walked over to the window and hung the medicine wheel. The leather strapping allowed it to dangle from the curtain rod above. I began thinking of the day's events and

Marcus Shikoba. A smile crossed my face as I gazed at his grandfather's gift. It was really nice to go out. It was the first day since I had been to Maine that I had a good time.

It was then that the strangest thing happened. I heard a large creaking sound. It was as if the entire room had settled all at once. It was a slight tremor, but it didn't make me lose my footing. I could feel the vibration under my feet from the floor boards below. I became filled with trepidation. I didn't like the sound and hoped that it wasn't an indication of the floor failing and giving way to the room below. The area groaned like it was in a state of agony. The shade that hung from the big window rolled up in frenzy, like someone had pulled the cord and made it retract. It continued to spin around and around. When it was completely rolled up, it stopped. I laughed in embarrassment, trying to brush off the jitters that I felt. I walked up and touched the medicine wheel again.

When I think back on the events after that day, I wish I had known then what I know now. I would have done things differently. If I hadn't seen those things for myself, I would have never believed it. It's weird how a person's perception and beliefs can change by one single incident. That day was that last day my family and I had inner peace, for after that day, things got worse for my family and me.

Chapter 9

I woke up to the sound of the phone ringing. Rubbing my eyes, I looked over at my clock to see the time. The clock showed the time of five thirty a.m. I took the phone from its cradle. Before I could say hello, I heard my mother answer.

"Lauren it's me, Ivy."

I didn't recognize the voice. I looked at the time again. She had an accent just like Mother's. Out of curiosity, I decided to continue listening and not tell them that I was on the line also. Mother didn't say anything in reply.

"You can't keep my family from me, Lauren. It's not right. I want to see my kin."

"How did you get this number, Ivy?" Mom sounded angry when she asked the question.

"You know how. I would like to talk to our Amanda, please."

"You will do no such thing, Ivy. I forbid it."

"Do you think that our Lucas would approve of your decision?"

"I am doing what is best for my family."

"I am an old woman, Lauren. I would like to see you. The caravans have traveled a lot this year, and the business is very profitable. I could help, you know."

"I do not want or need any of your services."

"It breaks my heart to hear you talk like that, kid. Why don't you let our Amanda decide?"

The phone buzzed a bit. The connection wasn't a good one.

"You are not in a good place, Lauren. Something isn't right with the home you live in," the woman continued. "Amanda is like us, you know."

The woman's words enraged my mother even more. "Don't call here again. Do you hear me?"

My mother hung up the phone but I stayed on the line. I could hear the woman breathing steadily in the receiver. Something inside me wouldn't put the receiver down in its cradle. I was waiting, for what I don't know. Then the voice startled me. "Amanda, is that you?"

When the woman said my name, I quickly hung the phone up. I laid my head back on my pillow and placed my arm on my face to block out the hints of light peering through the open door to the hallway. My thoughts scattered, trying to figure out who the caller was. Mom never mentioned a woman named Ivy in conversation. I turned the phone over and scanned through caller ID. The number wasn't familiar, and by the looks of its digits, it was long distance. Mom seemed extremely disturbed by the caller. What was the big secret? She knew my name and my father's. That much was evident. Maybe there was family I had no knowledge of. But why didn't mother tell me about her? I felt foolish for hanging up the phone, but I didn't want to upset my mother any more than she was. I got up and looked out the hallway with caution. I softly moved my footing, trying not to make any noise.

When I arrived at my brother's door, I opened it and walked in. When I sat on his bed, he jumped up with an intake of breath.

"Jeez." Toby ran his hands across his face and then tried to focus his eyes on me. "What are you doing?"

"Toby, I think we have other family."

"What?" he asked as he reached out for the lamp to turn on the light.

"Someone named Ivy called this morning asking to see to us. She knew about Dad."

"Amanda, you came in here at," he looked up at the clock, "six in the morning to tell me that someone called Mom." Toby lay back down and slapped the pillow over his head.

I tried to grab it off his face. "I am serious. Aren't you curious at all about who it is?"

Toby opened one eye and looked at me. "Not at the moment, no." Toby pulled the pillow back onto his face and held it there with both hands.

I slapped the pillow hard, opened handed.

"Ouch."

"Well I am." I stood up and began to walk out.

"Amanda,"Toby shouted, trying to get my attention.

I continued to walk to my room and closed the door. It was Friday, and school was something I had to do.

I took the stairs two at a time. Mom greeted me at the bottom.

"Amanda, what are you doing?"

I smiled as I walked past her. "Checking the stairs' durability."

There it was again, that look of "don't lie to me."

I hugged the end of the banister. "Marcus wanted to take me to the lighthouse on Mount Desert Island. I was wondering if I could do that today." I gave Mom my innocent smile.

Mom's crossed arms were not a very good indication of an approval. "What about the carriage house?"

"I swear, if you let me go today, I am all yours this weekend." I clasped my hands together tightly like in a silent prayer as I promised her.

Mom's hesitation was killing me. Sometimes I felt like a puppet on a string.

With an exhale of breath, she allowed it. I hugged her, saying, "Thank you." I was so excited that I had not asked about the woman on the phone. Thinking back on it, I wish I had.

Mom decided to drop us off at school. I was happy it was Friday, and if the truth was to be told, I was eager to see Marcus again. My mother pulled me from my thoughts.

"Amanda, I want you to stop at the house before you go out. I would like to meet the boy."

I smiled, waving my hand. "Okay, I'll see you after school."

Toby and I walked to the main doors. I stopped in midstride when I thought I had seen something moving on the roof of the high school. I placed my open hands over my eyes to try to get a better look.

"Amanda, what you looking at?" Toby asked from behind me.

When I turned to answer him, the person was gone. "I thought I saw someone on the roof."

Toby just shrugged it off. "Probably a roofer checking the singles, that's all."

"Yes, you're probably right."

I shook off the feeling and entered the building.

Time at school was going very slowly today. Why is that when you have something to do, the hours just slowly tick by? I continuously stared at the clock. I called Marcus while I was on lunch break to see if he wanted to see me today. He agreed, offering to pick Daphne and me up after school. I decided it would be best if we met him outside the school gates to avoid problems.

I was walking to my locker after lunch when I saw Cheryl and a few of her friends in the hallway. They were so engrossed with what was going on they didn't see me coming. I could hear the laughing and the goading. I walked over to see what was going on in the center of it all. I tried to break the circle by pushing my weight through the crowd. When I finally arrived, I couldn't believe what I saw. To my dismay, it was Cheryl coloring Daphne's face with lipstick. I pushed the last girl aside as I broke it up. I grabbed Cheryl's arm before she could put another mark on Daphne's face.

"That's enough, Cheryl."

Cheryl seemed surprised that it was me. She quickly recovered and gave me a serene look. "Who are you, her mother?"

I tried to control my anger, but enough was enough. I grabbed Cheryl's shoulders. It was like my hands had a mind of their own. I pushed her into the lockers. Holding her steadfast with my open palms pressed on her shoulders, I whispered, "No, I am not her mother, but I'll tell you who I am. I am the girl that will rip your face off the next time you come near her again. Do you understand?" I pushed her into the lockers again to make my point.

Cheryl pushed back. Before I knew it, the pushing turned into other things. Cheryl hit me. I hit her back, right in the face. She seemed blinded by the punch but still got her own hit in. I still didn't know how she managed it. We both went down to the floor like a sack of potatoes. I heard the sound of the principal's voice in the cheering crowd. As the principal grabbed us both to separate us, the bell rang, and the sea of people scattered into their classrooms. Cheryl and I remained with Daphne still on the ground.

"You'll regret that," Cheryl screamed with venom in her voice.

"Can't wait," I responded with a sly smile.

The principal, Mrs. Goad, shook us both by the arms as she held us in a tight grip. "That's enough."

Cheryl was the first to be released. She staggered as she took her books in her arms. When Mrs. Goad freed me from her grasp, I walked over to Daphne.

I looked down and helped her up. "Are you okay?"

Daphne was humiliated, I could tell. She pushed her glasses up to the bridge of her nose so she could see me better. When I looked at her face, I wanted to punch Cheryl all over again. She didn't take my hand right away, but she did eventually. I stared at Daphne, waiting for some explanation.

"So what is going on here, girls?" Mrs. Goad asked with impatience. The only reply was silence.

Daphne shrugged and whispered in my ear, "Cheryl said she was going to decorate my face in the same fashion as my ancestors."

I had a few tissues in my purse and gave them to her. "Do you want to tell?" I asked as she took the tissues.

"No, it just makes things worse."

I nodded in understanding.

"Thank you, Amanda," Daphne whispered again.

I just nodded in response.

"Daphne," Mrs. Goad began, "What happened to your face?"

"Nothing, Mrs. Goad. It's just a misunderstanding, that's all."

I nodded again, putting my arm around her.

"Okay, since no one wants to talk about it, we'll just take this down to my office until someone does."

Daphne pointed to my bottom lip. "You're bleeding."

I wiped the small droplets from my face. "Lucky shot." Who was I kidding? It hurt like crazy, but I wouldn't give Cheryl the satisfaction of knowing that fact.

Daphne was a barrier between us, once we were seated in the principal's office. I couldn't help looking over Daphne in Cheryl's direction. Her left eye already started to show signs of a shiner. She placed the bag of ice over her eye in an attempt to conceal it from me. I started to feel better already. I sat deeper in my chair.

We were in the office for about an hour, sitting in silence. Mrs. Goad lost her patience and decided to give us all detention next Monday. As we all stood up, Cheryl shoved past me. "See you around, Mandy."

"You bet you will." I smiled with a sneer.

Mrs. Goad halted me in my tracks. "Amanda, not you."

I flinched when I heard my name. Cheryl laughed as she walked out of the room.

Mrs. Goad came from behind and closed the door.

"Please sit."

I sat, waiting for whatever was to come. She looked mean and tough. I didn't think she was going to let me off lightly. She looked down at a file and then looked back up at me. "Amanda, we in this institution don't take violent acts lightly." She reclined in her chair slowly. "However," she said as she twirled her pen in her left hand, "one of the teachers stated that you came in Daphne's defense." She stood up quickly, crossing her arms behind her back as she walked over to the window. "Cheryl and Daphne have had conflicts in the past. I have decided to overlook this incident. Please don't make me regret it."

Mrs. Goad looked over her shoulder at me to see my reaction. I just nodded in compliance.

"Good," she said as she walked over to her office and opened the door to let me go. After I left, she closed the door quickly behind me. My insides curled. I knew that she would call my mother sooner or later. I was hoping that it would later. I really wanted to see Marcus.

Chapter 10

Daphne wanted to take the bus to her grandfather's. After the day she had, she didn't want to go out with Marcus and me. When he arrived, I was eager and nervous at the same time. I didn't know much about him, but in a way, it made everything more interesting and adventurous. I didn't know if it was a smart thing to do, but my curious nature got the best of me when he said he wanted to show me something.

I was surprised when Marcus did appear. He didn't bring the car. It was his motorcycle. I figured Daphne had called him to tell him she wasn't coming, or it was planned by her from the start. I was glad my mother didn't see this picture. She definitely wouldn't approve of this.

The wind picked up, swirling below my feet. I could feel the coldness between my toes, but I welcomed the breeze, for my face was flushed. When he stopped before me, he removed his helmet. He smiled as he reached out behind himself and grabbed a second helmet. I could feel the butterflies in my stomach when he held out the protective gear in his hand. With shaky hands, I took it and placed it on my head. He then playfully tapped the top of the helmet with the heel of his hand. "Got to make sure it's securely on," he said with a smile. I laughed as he helped me onto the back of the bike. He revved the engine as I placed my arms around his middle, trying to lock my fingers together. He laughed as he felt my grip tighten when we started to drive off. I squeezed my eyes like we were about to take off in flight. I had never been on a bike before, and to be truthful, I was a bit nervous about it.

I was surprised that he didn't try to show off by speeding away. He actually drove slowly and steadily. I could feel his breathing under the palms of my hands. His chest raised and lowered in a calm, steady rate. In a way it helped me relax more, knowing he was comfortable. I liked being on the motorcycle. It made the ride feel more personal and free. I watched the trees blend into one color as he slowly picked up speed. He did this when he felt my tense body relax a bit. I could tell he was laughing when he shook his head from side to side.

"Where are we going?" I shouted through the helmet and the wind.

"You'll see," was all he said as he yelled back.

"I have to stop at home first. My mother wants to meet you."

He looked over his shoulder briefly and shouted, "Do you think she'll approve?"

"The bike, no. You, yes."

After I said that, he purposefully increased his speed so I would hold him tighter. When we arrived at the house, I had him park the bike at the cast iron gates, and we walked the rest of the way to the house. I was surprised my mom was actually home. I guess she really wanted to meet him. I only hoped that my mother wouldn't embarrass me in front of him. Of course we found her in the kitchen. She was cooking chicken soup. I could smell the food from the hallway. It was one of my favorites. I didn't want to walk in, but the sweet smell of chicken was beckoning me inside.

Marcus could tell that I was hesitant. It still bothered me to walk into the kitchen. He took my hand and squeezed it in reassurance as we walked in. "He's gone, Amanda. It's okay." He knew why I hesitated. I shivered, and Marcus rubbed my arms slowly to warm me.

Mom was at the granite island cutting celery. Mom stopped in mid stroke before cutting the next batch of veggies. I rolled my eyes to the heavens and prayed for strength. She smiled as she wiped her hands on her apron. She held her hand out and then shook Marcus's hand.

"Hello, Mrs. Pennington."

She smiled sadly. "Ms. Pennington, love." She continued after taking a brief look at me. "Amanda's father is no longer with us."

"Oh," he responded in surprise. "I am sorry. I had no idea."

Mom changed the subject. "You must be Marcus."

She looked back down and handled the carrots next.

While she was cutting them, she asked me to go get a jacket of my own for later. I didn't want to leave the room, but I knew that Mom wanted to be alone with him. I slowly walked away, giving Mom the sign language of behaving herself when Marcus wasn't looking. I left the room reluctantly. It seemed all was well so far. It didn't seem as though the principal called yet. I just hoped she didn't embarrass me.

"So, Marcus, where do you plan on going?"

Marcus gave his best smile when he said, "The lighthouse."

Mom cut some more. "Are you in Amanda's school?"

Marcus cleared his throat. "No, Amanda knows my sister, Daphne. That's how we know each other."

"Really?" She started to cut again. "I would like Amanda home by eight o'clock."

"Yes, Ms. Pennington. I will make sure that she's home."

"I should hope so." She thought for a moment. "Your father, is his name Trent?"

"Yes," he said in a quick response.

"I saw your dad at the gallery in town yesterday. He's a very nice man. He had a lot of questions about Amanda. He seemed very interested about the extent of your relationship."

Mom could tell by Marcus's blush that he was embarrassed by what his father had done.

"It's in his nature to be intrusive. I am sorry about

that." Marcus didn't know what else to say.

"Oh, it's okay, Marcus. It doesn't bother me a bit. It shows he cares."

Mom placed her hands on her hips when she saw me walk back into the kitchen.

"I will see you two later then, Amanda."

I nodded in return and quickly grabbed Marcus's arm to get him out as quickly as I could. "I don't know what was said, but I hope she wasn't too harsh."

His smile seemed like a good sign. I said good-bye, and we left the house.

I was surprised when we arrived at the lighthouse. I removed the protective gear from my head so I could hear the roaring sea better. Marcus then did the same. I loved the smell of the ocean. The sky gave out some yellows and reds that highlighted the sun.

He took my hand in his and led me close to the edge of the reef. Marcus stared out into the distance and began speaking as though he were talking to someone else. "In Maine there are less than one percent of my people still here. The ones that survived the siege left because of too much change." He then turned to look at me. "Aki wanted me to show you something. I don't know why or for what reason."

I began to laugh to brush off the wave of nervousness. "What could you possibly show me on the edge of a cliff?"

Marcus turned to me fully and shook his head. "It's not

what's on the edge of the cliff, but what is below it." He could tell by my look that I was confused by his answer. "I can't explain it. I have to show you."

We started to walk off as he spoke. "Aki has always brought me here since I was young. I come here a lot when I need to be alone. When I was a bit younger, I was angry and careless and made a lot of bad choices."

I stopped walking, and he followed my lead. "Like doing the jump at West Point?"

"Yeah, like doing the jump." He walked again. "I don't know what you've heard about me. Some things are probably true; a lot of it isn't. I guess what I am trying to say is..." he fumbled, trying to find the right words. "I don't want you to get the wrong idea about me. I am not what people say I am."

"I am a big girl, and I can make decisions for myself. Besides, I am not one that listens to gossip. Let me rephrase that. I listen to it, but I don't believe things I hear."

Marcus shoved his hands in his pockets. "I am glad."

I couldn't help smiling. I could tell he felt awkward about the discussion. "Besides, I don't need to know your past history. The past should be left where it is."

He nodded his head in agreement. We halted at a narrow path, and he held his hand out, gesturing me to walk first. I could feel him right behind me as I walked on the path. He held my arm as I moved down the steep incline to the edge of the beach that appeared through the trees. I playfully grabbed the sand in my hand and felt its texture as it slid through my fingers. I turned to him and grinned like a little child. I eagerly took my shoes off and dug my feet into the soft, white sand. My toes sunk in deep as I inhaled the fresh, salty air. Marcus took my hand in his and guided me back to the cliffs.

"You may want to put your shoes back on. Once we get to the rocks, we will have to do some climbing."

The ocean's fierce waves crashed against the rocks and then left as fast as it came. The volcanic rock stood poised before us, daring us to scale its rough surface. As I followed the bluff's outline, I noticed the raindrops that started to fall. Marcus took off his leather jacket and placed it around my shoulders. I looked up again. "I don't think I can make that climb."

"It's not as far as you think," Marcus said as he stood behind me. He walked past and started to move in between the rocks.

I looked upward one more time before I heard his voice.

"Come on, Amanda."

As I walked into the small void between the cold stones, I could hear the echo of the water forcing its way through the massive boulders. The basalt rock's dark color made the scenery appear portentous. As I wandered through the maze I could still hear Marcus calling me. My heart was pounding as hard as the water against the rocks. I found it terrifying and exhilarating at the same time. For me I was walking through uncharted waters, and my only beacon was Marcus. I loved the water and the open sea, but this was taking it to the limit. I feared that at any time Mother Nature could send a strong wave that could take us both out to sea. After a few minutes, I finally found the opening that was naturally carved deep into the rock face. I slowly walked into the dark space and began whispering Marcus's name.

"I am here; keep walking."

"I don't have a flashlight," I called out.

"You won't need one."

I saw another opening that was much smaller than the first. It seemed that a blue fluorescent light pulsated from the rock's cavities. It was as though the light called me to it. It was hard not to be curious and stare at what caused this luminosity. As I moved closer to the opening, I was amazed to see the entire cave light up. The bioluminescence was incredible. It was like another world under the one we know. That's when I heard Marcus speak out. "There, glow worms. They live on the ceiling of the cave and attract insects inside. The brighter the light, the hungrier they are."

"It's amazing," was all I could say. I had never seen such a sight. Who would have thought that God's creation of beauty would be tucked away in darkness, surrounded by stone? In the center of the cave I could see a small pool of water. As the light source continued, it gave the water an aqua color. It was such a deep blue. The color reminded me of Marcus's eyes. There were also tons of stalactites that hung above us. The light illuminated the mineral's colors and made them glow in fluorescence of their own design. "It's beautiful." The reds, yellows, and greens on the minerals defined their bright colors. I could stay there forever.

I could see a set of stairs carved into the rocks, and they ascended to a second floor. I looked around and took in all the surroundings. I walked into the center of the room and placed my hands in the cold pool that rested in secrecy. The water was so clear I could see all the marine life that lived inside. Even when I cupped the liquid in my hands, it still gave its dark blue color. I stayed on bent knee taking in the brilliance of it all.

Marcus walked over beside me. "Aki said you would like it."

"Do all the kids come here?"

Marcus's expression changed quickly. "No," Marcus stated flatly. "No one is to know this is here, and I am asking you not to tell anyone."

"Why?"

"For a lot of reasons. For one, Aki trusts you enough to keep the secret."

I looked at him as I asked, "And what about you? Do you trust me?"

Marcus never responded. He walked away, and I followed him up another level into an adjoining cavern.

"Hey, you didn't answer..." I stopped as I looked at the walls. "My question," I finished in a whisper.

On the walls were paintings and some sort of writings that I could not decipher. I went to touch the works of art, but Marcus took my hand. "You can't touch it. It's very old. This place is like a library of information that dates back to the origins of our people. This," he pointed around for effect, "is the cave of creation. Here is where my people started and how we came to be. The cave helps us remember who we are and the events that have occurred. That's why this place is a secret."

"This could be preserved better in a museum," I added.

Marcus scoffed. "They would just come here to take the relics, and they would damage everything else with it. This is one of the reasons why my family ensured that the property stayed in our hands."

"I still think—"

Marcus turned and grabbed my arms. "Listen. Don't think. This is important to me and my family. It's our secret."

I smiled slightly. "I won't tell anyone. Don't worry." I rubbed my shoulders to get warm. "It's like nothing I have ever seen."

I couldn't believe all the writing on the walls. It stretched all across the cavern. It was as if Marcus could read my mind when he said, "The caverns are vast. They are said to run underground for miles."

I smiled. "Have you wandered that far?"

Marcus smiled. "Like I said, they run for miles. One could get lost."

I guess I had my answer. I drew my attention back to the cave writings. "Can you read it?"

Marcus looked at me from the corner of his eye. "Yes"

I sat down on a boulder and stared at him with impatience. "Well, don't just stand there. Read and teach me something."

He shoved his hands in his pockets. "I didn't bring you here for a lesson."

"Okay, then what did you bring me here for?"

"I told you. Aki asked me to."

"But you didn't have to." I jumped off the stone and landed on my feet. I walked over to the wall again. I continued to look at the wall. "What's this word?"

Marcus stood next to me and said, "*Shilup Chitoh Osh* , this is the word for the Great Spirit."

I tried to say it, but I was pronouncing it wrong. He grabbed my bottom jaw hoping to help me say it correctly. After a few times, I couldn't help laughing. He looked so serious when he said the word, and I was only playing. I could have said it right the first time around, but he didn't know it. Marcus started to caress my face with the back of his hand. I stopped laughing and looked as serious as he did.

He slowly moved closer to me and began to bring his face closer to mine. My breath shortened and my lips parted. I gripped onto his shirt front as our noses touched. I closed my eyes and waited. Waited. But nothing happened. All I heard was the slight whisper of Marcus saying, "*Shilup Chitoh Osh* ."

When I opened my eyes, he smiled when he saw my look of disappointment. He adjusted his jacket tighter around me. He frowned when he noticed the slight bruising of my bottom lip. His thumb gently traced the wound. He quickly dropped his hand down, realizing that he lingered too long, and whispered something. I wasn't sure what he said, but I knew it wasn't good. He looked back up at me with a look of hopelessness. "Daphne told me what you did."

I didn't say a word. All I did was nod in response.

As I looked downward, Marcus placed his hand under my chin, raising my eyes back up to look at him. "Thank you," he said in the awkward silence.

I licked my lips in a nervous act. I grinned a bit as I said, "I am not at all sorry about it. I'd do it again."

Marcus exhaled quickly. "Daphne has a hard time making friends. People don't understand her. That's the only thing I hate about not being in that school. I can't be there for her." He gave a charming, boyish smile. "I am glad she has you." He took my hand in his.

I was at a loss for words. I never had any boy talk to me

the way Marcus did. I shivered a bit, and he stepped closer. "It is a bit cold isn't it?" I asked nervously.

I felt as skittish as a horse. I didn't know what to expect or what to do. He was so close, and I thought for a moment he was going to kiss me. I wanted him to, but was afraid. He cradled my face in his hands once again. He brought his face close to mine again and whispered. "Aki was right about you."

My head was so clouded with other thoughts that it wasn't registering what Marcus Shikoba said. I didn't care what he was saying. I just nodded again.

"I trust you," he whispered. He backed away.

I felt as though I had lost my breath. I was surprised and shocked at the same time. I was angry at myself for letting him do that to me. I didn't like what I was feeling.

Marcus dragged me from my thoughts when he spoke. "Come on. It's getting late. I think it's time to take you home."

When we arrived home, Marcus didn't kiss me. All he said was goodnight. I hoped I hadn't done something that had upset him; then again he didn't seem troubled. I thought I gave all the right signals. I handed his helmet back to him. I hugged him as I said thank you and goodnight, and he hugged me back. As he drove off, my thoughts wandered on the events of the day. I was hoping I didn't do something to put him off. Maybe he just wanted to take things a bit slower. I started to wave as he disappeared into the distance.

Chapter 11

Marcus drove down Sound Drive. The sea was still in the distance. The evening was cool, but at least the rain died down. Marcus's thoughts were interrupted as he pulled onto Abel Lane. He pulled his motorcycle into the driveway and peered up at the window with the light that was still on. He watched the curtain sway side to side. He wasn't sure if it was Daphne or his father. He sighed slightly before he got off his bike. He hoped that it was Daphne waiting for him, but his instincts told him otherwise. Marcus took his time as he approached the front door. He knew what was waiting for him on the other side. He jingled his keys in the palm of his hand, questioning if he should walk in or leave again.

Marcus turned the key in the door and walked inside. He quickly removed his coat and placed his keys on the kitchen counter. He could smell a hint of cherry in the air. It was the scent of his fathers cigar. He knew the brand well, for his dad smoked them often. Marcus put his jacket in the closet.

"Marcus!"

Trent Shikoba walked from the shadows smoking a cigar as he confronted his son. Trent and Marcus were almost identical in looks. Marcus was just a younger version. Trent's chocolate brown eyes gave out an accusing glare.

Marcus knew what was coming.

Trent removed his cigar slowly from his mouth and stared at it as he chose his words carefully. "I spoke with your employer."

Marcus didn't give any indication of uneasiness. Instead he crossed his arms in defiance.

His father continued, "He tells me that you left work early today."

Marcus finally found his voice. "I am sorry that my leaving work early doesn't meet your approval," he stated with a voice filled with sarcasm.

"Marcus, you know it's not that. Even though you have been released early, you know that there are certain attachments to that liberty. Your probation officer will not approve."

Marcus started to walk away.

"Daphne tells me you met a girl named Amanda." That comment made Marcus stop in his tracks. "She tells me she's a nice girl. She also tells me that the family moved into 210 Water Street. I had the pleasure of meeting her mother the other day."

"So I have heard."

Marcus watched his dad intently. His father still dressed in his black slacks and white dress shirt. Trent walked over to the liquor cabinet and began to pour himself a drink. Trent's dark hair was usually in a small ponytail, but it was loose, leaving his hair down to his shoulders. "Did you take her to see the old man?"

"Yes."

"I am assuming that he hasn't a clue where the girl lives. You know about the land they live on. Your grandfather wouldn't like it if he knew." When he finished his sentence, Trent took the liquid into his mouth quickly and swallowed.

Marcus began to move again, clenching his fists to his sides.

"Marcus, I don't want to fight with you. I just don't want you traveling down the wrong road."

"How would you know what road I am traveling these days, when you're never around to see it for yourself?"

"I have my work, Marcus. I am doing my best. I did all this," he pointed to their surroundings, "for you and your sister."

Marcus ran his fingers through his hair in frustration. "This conversation is over," Marcus said with a laugh.

Trent had enough of the disrespect. "I will say when a conversation is over in my house."

Marcus turned to face his father again. "You're always at work. That's your life, not ours. Aki has always been there for us. You haven't. Even when she left, he was there. You were too concerned about yourself to even think how we felt or how much we hurt. You buried yourself in work and hid away from us when we needed you most."

"She has a name, and she is your mother. Regardless of the mistakes she has made, she is still your mother." Trent's cigar blazed a cherry red as the smoke filled the room. Marcus knew that even though his mom had done the things she did, his father still loved her. "I am here now, Marcus. Doesn't that count for something? You can't continue to live in the past. It will eat you up inside until there is nothing left but hate. Don't hate me, Marcus. I am not the enemy here."

"Where's Daphne?" Marcus asked, trying to change the subject.

"Asleep."

Marcus was at the foot of the stairs.

"Marcus?"

"Yes?"

"I am here for you, always am. I just want you to know that."

Marcus still didn't respond.

"Don't be late for work tomorrow," was the last think his father said.

Marcus looked back and Trent was gone. Marcus did feel a bit guilty for the way he treated Trent. If it weren't for his father's talent in the trade, Marcus would still be in a detention home. He knew his father cared, but he still resented him for the mistakes he had made.

Even though Trent thought Marcus was the same,

he wasn't. Marcus was lost and wild at one time, but being away from his family and life gave him a different perspective. He wished that Trent could see that. He was an angry, lost soul, but he was tired of being angry. He wanted to move on. Marcus had not spoken to his mother in eight years. She had never attempted to call, let alone write them. There was no explanation for her actions. Nothing.

The room that once held her belongings was empty. It was Trent's connections that tracked his mother down, finding that not only was she still alive, but also that she had left the country and gone back to her family in Ireland. Marcus was ten years old at the time she left, and he had grown bitter. Daphne was only eight at the time. A daughter needed her mother, and she had abandoned her. That was when Joshua came into the picture. He and Marcus became best friends and had been until Marcus got into trouble. That was when Marcus realized how bad Joshua really was. In truth, it was Joshua who destroyed Nathan's car. Marcus took the fall only so Joshua wouldn't lose his scholarship for college. He already had a reputation as a bad boy. Marcus knew that with his father being a lawyer, he would get a better deal. Marcus served time and Joshua not only walked scot free, but also made Marcus realize how a friend can stab him in the back. It was too late to tell about Joshua's past. Marcus served the time, and no one would believe him anyway. He swore he would never do anything like that for anyone again. Joshua was not the friend that Marcus thought he was.

Marcus didn't understand what compelled Joshua to attack him. He could tell that Joshua wasn't even interested in Amanda until Marcus had shown an interest. He also knew that eventually he and Josh would collide. It was only a matter of time. Amanda was different from the other girls that Marcus had gone out with. He liked that. She spoke her mind and had a strong spirit. Marcus's grandfather surprised him when he took to Amanda. Maybe he felt what Marcus did. It was like an energy that drew you in. Marcus couldn't explain it. It was like she had a special aura about her. People gravitated to her. Aki's words were still haunting Marcus, "She is right for you. You will grow to need her." Marcus closed his eyes tightly, trying to forget Aki's words.

He tried to turn his thoughts in another direction as he finished his climb to the top of the stairs. That was when Marcus got a call.

I sat in my bed thinking of the day's events. The caverns were a great wonder. I clasped my hands behind my head and stared at the ceiling above. Taboo jumped on me, purring. She then tried to get comfortable on my chest, digging her claws into my front.

"Ouch," I pushed her over to my side and stroked her

thick fur.

I turned my head slightly when I heard a noise by the window. Out of curiosity, I stood up to see what it was. When I moved closer to the window, I noticed that the medicine wheel was lying on the floor. I picked it up and moved to the window to hang it back up. When I was done with my task, I looked at the glass window. I thought I saw a reflection in the doorway. It was small, like a child. I looked at the doorway, and it was empty. The light in the hallway began to flicker on and off. Taboo was lying on the bed and began hissing loudly. She growled and hissed as her fur stood on end. The light flashed on and off like a strobe light. I picked up the cat as I moved into the hallway. I tried to calm her as well as myself, but it wasn't working. The cat began to fight, warning me to release my hold on her. When her nails dug deep into my skin, I let her go. She fell, landing feet first. The Siamese retreated under the bed, leaving me alone in the hallway. The walls seemed to have outlines of shadows that moved and undulated until they disappeared into the plaster.

The hallway light began to get brighter and brighter as I went to the bulb to see it better. I heard a high-pitched sound that seemed to be generating from the it. As I stood directly beneath the bulb, I heard a pop. The light went out, and the shattering glass of the bulb followed. The pieces scattered, falling on my head as I covered myself. I felt the glass pierce the skin on my arms and hands. I shouted as I felt the pain. I screamed in the hallway in the dark until I saw a figure.

The blood began to run down my arms. "MOM!"

My hands were shaking. I could still feel the glass in my skin.

"Toby?"

The figure came closer. I could feel the hairs on the back of my neck stand up. A wave of nausea overtook me. I crawled toward the light that was still coming from my room. When I saw the amount of blood, I began to gag. I could hear the sound of footsteps. The figure in the darkness came closer. For some reason, it redirected itself and collided with the wall. The silhouette then disappeared. I could feel the vibrations of the floor beneath my palms, and I tried to raise myself up to stand. I convinced myself that I was hallucinating. I stood fully and then staggered to the light at the doorway to my room. It was then that I heard a screech in the darkness. It sounded like a thousand birds were in the hall. It was then I felt the push. I jerked forward, falling onto the floor unexpectedly. My face hit the wood planks hard. A rush of breath escaped my lips as I hit the floor with force. I tried to crawl into my room to escape the attacker. A hard tug on my leg pulled me backwards. I didn't react quickly, still dazed by the initial fall. Taboo ran to me as I was pulled farther into the darkness. I tried to hold myself by digging my nails into the hardwood floor. My breathing was fast. The fright I felt was indescribable. In a panic I began swinging my arms around as I was pulled deeper into the darkness. I was in a state of complete shock as I tried to scream. Taboo was still close to me hissing at the unknown.

I tried to kick my feet in hopes of a quick release, but it was no use. I couldn't see anyone. I was pulled in farther as I screamed for help. I could feel the wood splinters in my skin and under my fingernails. I could feel my body weaken as the struggle continued. Taboo hissed, baring her teeth. With one more growl, the cat lunged behind me, disappearing into the dark void. I was released and moved into the light. I screamed for Toby. The last thing I saw was a pair of brown eyes looking into mine, and all went dark.

Chapter 12

Lauren Pennington sat in the waiting room of the hospital. Toby sat next to her and watched as she steepled her hands in prayer. She removed the tear that came down her cheek and then started wringing her hands as she waited for the doctor to come for her. When she had found Amanda, she was lying on the floor unconscious. Her arms were cut badly, and the bruises on her face were visible.

Lauren sat in silence. She stared at the floor and inhaled as she tried to stay calm. To her it seemed like hours. Marcus and Trent had just arrived when the doctors came out. Lauren stood quickly and greeted the doctors, asking if Amanda was all right.

"She's fine, Ms. Pennington. She may have a slight concussion from the fall. We had to stitch her left arm."

The doctors ushered Lauren into a private room to talk to her. They suggested that Marcus stay while they talked to Lauren alone. They closed the door and gestured for her to sit down. Lauren didn't have a good feeling.

"Ms. Pennington," the doctor began, "Have you ever known Amanda to hurt herself for any reason?"

"Excuse me?"

"Have you..."

"I heard the question," she said. "I just can't believe what I am hearing."

"Has she?"

"Of course not. Amanda would never do such a thing."

The other doctor took over the conversation. "Your daughter says that she was attacked, Ms. Pennington, but she could not tell us who it was."

Lauren sat quietly and folded her hands. "We had an intruder in the house a few weeks ago. I was gone for only half an hour. I went to the store." Lauren covered her eyes. "I should have been home."

"We believe that the marks are self-inflicted. Is her father here?"

Lauren said tiredly, "Her father is dead."

"I see," one of the men in a lab coat answered.

A police officer was also in the room. Lauren didn't hear him come in. "Your daughter claims that her father was at the house during the time of attack."

"That's impossible. She was probably confused."

"Perhaps." The police officer stretched out his hand to Lauren. "Officer Felding, Ms. Pennington."

She took his hand in hers.

He asked, "Was your daughter with anyone else tonight?"

"She was out with some boy named Marcus earlier. He left the house before I went out. "

Officer Felding looked at her. "Yes, we saw the Shikoba

boy with his father on the way in. Would you mind if I spoke to your daughter?"

With a nod of Lauren's head, the officer left to see Amanda.

Marcus had been sitting in the room for an hour. Trent sat beside him as they waited for Lauren to come out into the waiting room. Trent was surprised to see Officer Felding instead, walking in their direction.

"Mr. Shikoba?"

Trent stood up with Marcus and shook Officer Felding's hand. "Hey, Derek, what brings you here?"

"The Pennington girl was attacked in her home today."

Marcus sat down as Felding looked in his direction. "Can you tell me where you were at 9:30, Marcus?"

Marcus became defensive. "You've got to be kidding me." He stood up. "I was with Amanda most of the day and then I took her home around 8:00."

"And after that?"

Trent chimed in before Marcus could speak again. "He was with me, Derek, at home." Trent kept his hand on Marcus's chest, holding him at bay as he spoke to the officer.

Marcus looked at his dad and knew it was not the time to speak. Officer Felding looked at Trent's face, then at Marcus's and nodded his head. "Sorry, Trent. I have to do this."

Trent shoved his hands in his pockets. "I know."

"Marcus, did you notice anything usual when you dropped Amanda off this evening?"

Marcus ran his fingers through his hair and exhaled in frustration. "No, I can't say that I did. I only dropped her off. I didn't stay long."

"I was told by Lauren Pennington that the school called her after you and Amanda left the house this afternoon. She stated that there was an incident today at school involving Cheryl Thornhope, Daphne, and Amanda. Did Amanda say anything to you about it?"

Marcus shook his head. "Amanda didn't say much about it. Daphne mentioned something about the fight at school."

"Where is Daphne?"

"At home asleep," Trent stated.

He then looked at Trent. "Can I speak with you outside, Trent?"

Trent nodded his head in approval and walked with the policeman outside. Trent didn't wait to question once the automatic glass doors slid shut. "So what do you think?" he asked as they stood outside in the cold.

"I don't get paid to think. I get paid to find the answers."

Trent looked at Derek. "No one has been in that house since we were kids, and you remember what happened to that family."

Officer Felding nodded. "Yep, I remember. It's just a

house with a bad history, that's all. I don't believe in local folklore."

Trent ran his fingers through his hair in the same manner as Marcus did. "Geez, Derek. They found Mrs. Warwick dead in a crawl space in the basement."

"I still think the husband did it."

Trent stared at Derek as if he were daft. "He was in Rome, on business."

"Are you sure about that?"

Trent turned away for a second. "They should have demolished that house years ago. Does the family know about the place?"

"Your guess is as good as mine. Hopefully the realtor estate agents explained it. I believe that they have to disclose that information.

"Are they privy to that? I am not so sure. Statute provides that no action can be pursued against an agent. If the death had occurred more than three years prior to the date of sale, they walk clean. They don't have to disclose anything. Maybe you should say something, Derek. You are a cop."

"Oh, come on, Trent. I am sure the kids hear enough about it at school. You're an intelligent man. You don't actually believe in all that hocus pocus."

"My father does."

Derek stopped for a moment. "You know that's not what I meant. I respect your father. He's a good man."

"My father and I really haven't talked much since Catherine left. I guess in a way I was too proud to admit that he was right about her."

Derek changed the subject. "So how well does your son know the Pennington girl?"

"Well enough. I haven't met her, but Daphne likes her. She mentioned the fight that broke out today. Cheryl was teasing Daphne, and Amanda interceded."

"I haven't spoken to Cheryl Thornhope yet. I don't think she had anything to do with the attack, but you never know." After a brief pause he then said, "Why don't you have Daphne tell her about the house?"

Trent sighed. "She may have already. I'll talk with her." Trent then turned around and asked, "So what did Amanda say?"

"Trent, you know I can't discuss that with you."

"I heard from Marcus that there was an intruder in the house a few weeks ago."

"Trent, I can't confirm or deny."

Trent cut him off. "Do you really believe that it's kids playing pranks?"

Derek shook his head. He should have known that Trent was keeping a close eye on this one. He was talking to someone on the force. Derek couldn't blame him, though. It was Trent's kid, after all, who was interested in this girl.

"I'll see you around, Trent."

"Oh, yes, Derek. You will indeed."

Chapter 13

Lauren sat in the big office. When the secretary told her that the doctor was ready to see her, she started to question if she was doing the right thing. She sat in the leather chair waiting for the psychiatrist to start. The man looking down at his paperwork appeared to be in his mid-forties. The hospital suggested this course of action for Amanda. Lauren didn't want to do this, after what she had been through, but if it would help her, she was all for it. He took his glasses off and began the session.

"Mrs. Pennington, I am Doctor Gabe."

Lauren took the psychiatrist's hand for a shake. "Please call me Lauren. You wanted to have a session with me before you talked with my daughter?"

He adjusted his glasses. "Yes, I wanted to talk to you a bit about your daughter. Anything you can tell me about her. I wanted to know what I can about her family history."

Lauren began to wring her hands. "She's a good kid. Everything had been fine until we moved to Maine. Look, I am only here because the hospital wanted her evaluated. They feel that Amanda was inflicting pain on herself. I just want to make sure that she's okay." Lauren exhaled. "I didn't know what else to do."

"Are there any cases of mental illness that you know of in the family?"

Lauren began rubbing her face. She didn't know where to begin. She decided to just be blunt and get this session over with. "Amanda's father died when she was very young. She didn't know him."

The doctor just nodded as she continued.

"Her father, Lucas, was diagnosed with schizophrenia. Amanda doesn't know about it. I blame Lucas's family; they brainwashed him."

"How so?"

Lauren stood up and walked over to the opened window as she spoke. "In England, Lucas's family consisted of traveling caravans, trapeze artists, magicians, and so forth. They were part of a circus act. They were gypsies. His grandmother is a respected elder of the troop."

Lauren pulled out a cigarette. "Is it okay?"

The doctor nodded. "If it helps."

Lauren gazed out the opened window as if she were in a trance. Looking at the sky she began to recount the years with Lucas. She lit the end of the cigarette and inhaled. "I quit years ago. It's funny how stress can make you pick up old habits." She continued, "Lucas's grandmother had him convinced that he could see ghosts. She claimed she could. When I met Lucas, he was doing one of his shows. I didn't think that he actually believed that he could do all those things. It wasn't until a year later that I realized it. I always thought it was just part of an act."

"What did you do?"

"When I saw what was happening, I took him away from it all and convinced him to seek help. I was pregnant at the time. He said he would do it for me. Sometimes it seemed so real. At one time he almost convinced me."

The doctor rested his hand under his chin, while he listened intently. "Why would you say that?"

"People from different villages would come to see Lucas and his grandmother. It was very scary at times how exact he could be with the details. He always claimed that they looked just like you and me. Sometimes he said he couldn't tell the difference. When we went to the market one day, he started talking, but no one was there. No one was there," she said louder for effect.

"They, meaning who?"

"They were ghosts that he claimed to see."

"What about your husband's parents?"

"They died when he was a boy. His grandmother took him in and raised him."

Doctor Gabe tried to give Lauren a ray of hope. "As far as schizophrenia is concerned, Mrs. Pennington——" He corrected himself. "I mean Lauren, a child has only a twenty percent chance of inheriting the disorder from a parent. That is a very small number. First I will meet with Amanda, and then we will decide on a course of treatment." When he saw that his words offered some comfort, he continued.

"Have you seen any changes in your daughter lately?"

"Of course. She's in a new town, a new school. It's a big change for all of us." She looked at the doctor for guidance.

"And you. How are you holding up?"

"As best as expected, considering."

The doctor looked down at the paperwork. "It states here that your daughter had a violent episode a few weeks ago as well. An intruder attacked your daughter in your home?"

"Yes."

"Do you believe her?"

"I don't see why she would lie. She has never done anything like this before."

"Do you believe that your daughter inflicted those wounds on herself?"

"No," Lauren stated, quickly defending Amanda. "I saw the glass on floor. The light bulb did shatter."

"Has your late husband's family had any contact with you or Amanda?"

"No. She doesn't know my husband's family exists. That was not the life I wanted for any of us."

"Anything else you would like to add before our session is over?" Doctor Gabe waited patiently.

Lauren wanted her daughter to get well. She didn't want to hold back crucial information. "I am afraid, because my daughter truly believes that her father has been in that house. She claims that she has seen him, and that terrifies me."

The doctor stood up. "Maybe it would be best if we kept Amanda for a few days in our facility. This way I can have more time with her. I think that would probably be the best course of action at this time."

Lauren regretted it the minute she said it. She didn't know what the right thing was. All she knew was that she wanted her daughter to get well. "All right, I think a few days will be okay. Besides, it will get her out of that house." Lauren was praying she was doing the right thing as she signed the papers. She started to think hard. Time, she just needed a little time to think about everything. One thing was for certain. They were leaving that house.

Ivy was fretting. She quickly packed her bags and got on a plane. She had hired a private investigator months ago to track her family down. She had known where they lived for a few weeks. She didn't like the information that she was getting. The nightmare last night distressed her all the more. Something was wrong; she knew it; she could feel it. As she dreamt she saw her mother sitting by the river's edge as she always did when Ivy was a child. The scene was just as she remembered it. Ivy's mother was her guide to the other side. All seers had one. The guiding spirit in most cases was a family member. Her mother continued to dangle her feet over the boulder and move them around into the water below her. As Ivy walked closer, her mother turned, feeling her presence. Abby smiled, happy to see Ivy.

"I have been waiting for you. Where have you been?"

"You know, Mam. Clients, clients."

Her mother looked at her in disapproval. "You know it's never safe to channel without me. You take too many chances, Ivy. Always did."

"That was one trait that I hear I inherited from you."

Abby scoffed. "That's not the only thing you inherited, love, or we wouldn't be talking right now."

The wind started blow and the light was extinguished. "There's a storm coming, Ivy."

"I know."

"It's time to find the child."

"Mam she doesn't know me or our ways."

"She is like us."

Ivy shook her head. "I had a feeling it was our Amanda. I felt it when she was on the phone. I could feel the energy."

"She is misguided and needs you."

"Not according to her, mam."

Ivy's mother waved her hand over the water and gestured for Ivy to walk closer. "The house they reside in is no longer a lifeless unit. It feels her, Ivy. She's making things worse for herself by being in that place. There is too much hate and loss in that house. She's not ready for what she does not understand. The house knows. You need to go."

In the water's ripples, her mother showed her the day's events and the drastic measures her mother had taken in hopes of helping the child. "Mam, Lauren won't let me near her."

Abby placed her hand on Ivy's shoulder. "You have to try. Lauren will realize that you're there to help. The house will take the child in and feed on her until there is nothing left. Don't let this happen as it did with Lucas. Do not make the same mistake twice Ivy."

"Lucas was an adult, mam. He made his decision. I had to honor it."

"You haven't given Amanda a chance to decide for herself, and she is not an adult. She is still a child." Abby stated the fact.

"I know."

"And that's what makes her more in danger. The younger the life force, the stronger the energies within."

"Yes," Ivy agreed.

"She sees it, and it knows. So get up, lady, and take care of bloody business."

Ivy gazed at her mother one more time before she awakened from her slumber. The perspiration that beaded down her face moved down her throat onto her night dress. "Mother, you've always made a grand entrance and a timely exit."

Since four this morning, she had been making preparations. Ivy was now only waiting for the taxi. Once it arrived at her caravan, she looked inside its holdings again, for she knew that this time she may not come back.

Chapter 14

Marcus came to the door to see Amanda. Before he could knock, Lauren answered. She seemed surprised to see him.

"Is Amanda here?"

Lauren was reluctant to answer the question. She shook her head after a few moments. "I was on my way out, Marcus."

"I haven't seen her for a few days, and she's not answering her phone. Daphne says she hasn't been in school. Is she all right?" Marcus continued to follow Lauren after she locked the front door and continued walking down the porch stairs.

"Amanda is all right, Marcus. To be honest, she hasn't been home. I'll tell her you were here."

"Where is she?" Marcus was relentless.

"She doesn't want to see you right now, Marcus."

"Is she all right?"

Lauren eyed Marcus. "She's at the doctor's office."

"Can I go with you, Ms. Pennington?"

"I really don't think that's a good idea right now." Lauren got into the Volkswagen Beetle and tried to start the engine. The car wouldn't start. She turned the ignition key a few more times, but the car wouldn't fire. Lauren sighed in frustration and placed her head down on the steering wheel, praying for some kind of break.

Marcus smiled at Lauren. "Do you need a ride?"

"Marcus, she doesn't want to see anybody right now."

"I think maybe seeing me is what needs," he stated as he dangled the keys in front of her.

I sat in the quiet office of Doctor Gabe. I didn't like the medications they had put me on. The doctor thought it was best to give me some pills for depression. I was a bit depressed, but what teen wasn't? The medicine made things worse. I hated talking to the man. He was nice and all, but he didn't do a lot of talking, he just analyzed me. Anytime I was with him for the past week, I was always being very careful of what I was saying. The doctor was looking at paperwork as he spoke. "I had you fill out this questionnaire, Amanda, to help you, not to hurt you."

I just said "Hum, hum," in response.

He assessed the questionnaire again. "And did you answer the questions truthfully?"

"As truthfully as possible," I lied.

He placed his pen down on the paperwork in his lap. He then took his glasses off and rubbed his eyes lightly. "Okay then. Let's start with some small questions. Have you ever heard voices?"

SHADOWS

"Can you please define that? I mean the voices. If I hear a voice from an individual, that means that I am being spoken to, correct?"

I was surprised to see the man smile. "Amanda, you know what I mean."

I smiled. "I know. No, I do not hear voices."

"Have you seen your father in your home?"

I watched him carefully. "I told you, Dr. Gabe, that I lost a lot of blood. It was only a hallucination." I told him what he wanted to hear.

"Amanda, I can't help you if you won't let me. Tell me how you feel."

"I feel a lot of things, Dr. Gabe."

"Okay, right now, how do you feel?"

If he wanted to know how I felt right now, I figured I would tell him the truth. "I don't like to be analyzed. I feel like I am a prisoner here. I am attacked in my home by some guy that the police can't find. A bulb explodes in my hallway cutting my arms because I was trying to protect my face. Now I am in a room with a psychiatrist who is asking me how I feel. Let me ask you, doctor, how would you feel?"

"Angry."

"More frustrated than angry, but close enough."

"Okay, Amanda. I think our session is done for today," he added. The doctor was with me for a full hour. I could tell he was feeling like we were getting nowhere.

"Thank you," was all I could say.

"Amanda, can you wait in the hallway while I have a word with your mother?"

"Sure, Dr. Gabe."

I left the room, unsure of what was being said behind closed doors.

Lauren came in, and the doctor was amazed and baffled at the same time. He didn't know where to begin. "After being with Amanda for this week, I have found her delightful, but also I thought there were a few things that we should discuss."

It was just as Lauren feared.

Dr. Gabe smiled as he began, "The first day that Amanda was here, we gave her an IQ test and an MMPI. I was fascinated by her IQ scores. Amanda scored at one hundred forty, which is extremely high. This kind of intelligence is found in only about two percent of the population. The other test was called the Minnesota Multiphasic Personality Inventory. This test is used to define a person's personality and mental status. All in all, the test came out well." He then conjectured, "A little too well, for my taste. I can see that she suffers from depression, but otherwise she seems to be in perfect mental health."

Lauren digested the information and then asked, "What do you mean by the tests came out a little too well?"

Dr. Gabe cleared his throat. "The test is designed to prevent a person from dishonestly answering the questions. Taking into consideration Amanda's high IQ scores, this could be the reason for the clean bill of mental health. In other words, I don't believe she filled out the test truthfully."

Lauren sat back deeper in the chair and contemplated. "Amanda has always excelled in her academics. I never thought she was a genius."

"She is extremely intelligent. Amanda is at a higher level of intelligence than the average person. I wouldn't necessarily call her a genius, though."

Lauren moved closer to Dr. Gabe. "Are you sure about that?"

Dr. Gabe ignored the statement and continued, "I am not quite done with my analysis of the subject, but I assure you."

Lauren cut the doctor off. "Dr. Gabe, my daughter is not a test subject. She is a person and should be treated as such."

"I meant no——."

"I am sorry, Dr. Gabe, but I will be taking my daughter home today. I should have known better than to leave her in this place. I won't do it again."

Lauren stood up to leave. "I believe that we are finished here, Doctor."

As Lauren left to open the door, the doctor called to her one more time. "Are you sure that taking her back home will improve her mental state? Things may get worse."

Lauren turned in his direction and eyed him cautiously. "That will be something that I will have to live with, Doctor. Besides, according to you, she is in an excellent mental state. Good day."

"Are you aware that your mother-in-law has been here trying to see Amanda? I didn't let her see the girl, because of our past discussions. I told her that she needed your permission."

"Well, Dr. Gabe, at least that was one thing you've done right." Lauren was alarmed that Ivy was so close.

Before Lauren could escape, the doctor said, "Before you go, Lauren, I would like to have a discussion with you about Toby."

"What?" Lauren let go of the handle and decided to listen.

I sat in the waiting room on the edge of my seat. I didn't want to stay at the facility anymore. Some of the kids there were catatonic or rocked back and forth mumbling inaudible words. I shuttered as I thought of where I had been for the past week. I didn't want to go back here again, but at the same time, I worried. I questioned my sanity and what I had seen. I felt all right and sane, but don't most of the insane say the same thing? I didn't know if I was doing the right thing by not talking about what I thought happened. I knew if I did, I would never leave this place. I watched the rain again falling against the window pane. Pitter patter, pitter patter was all I could hear. The world was quiet, but Mother Nature was not. I was exhausted and depressed. My eyes filled with large tears as I continued to watch out the window beside me. The tears fell down my cheeks at a slower pace than the storm outside. I missed California. I wanted to go home. Everything was fine before we came to this place. I pulled my cardigan closer to myself for warmth and shivered at the thought of being here any longer than I had to.

As I looked out into the rain, I thought I saw someone staring at the window from the outside. She was an elderly woman with white, long hair. She had many bracelets on her wrists and a long skirt that almost touched the ground. Her apparel was very like her bracelets, brightly colored and odd. She looked at me, not breaking eye contact. It felt as though her brown eyes pierced me, seeing through me. She raised her right arm out toward me as I placed my open palm on the cold glass. I had seen her before, but where? She knew me; I could tell. I racked my brain, staring out into the storm that the stranger was surrounded by. Where did I see her before? She smiled, and then I turned. The sound of the slamming door brought me back from my thoughts.

Mom looked at me and took my hand. I could see the disdain on her face. She began to speak to me as I stood up. "Come on, Amanda. It's time to go home."

I smiled slightly and turned back to the window. The woman was gone.

My mother touched my shoulder to gain my attention. "Is something the matter, love?"

"No," I decided not to tell. "Nothing is wrong. Let's go home."

I didn't know that Marcus and Daphne had come with Mom. Mom had asked them to wait in the car to save me some of the embarrassment that I felt about the situation. It was nice to see friends. I hadn't seen Toby. I figured he was still at home finishing out his sentence.

But home wasn't where I ended up. Instead, I was at the home of Grandfather Shikoba. My first day out, I didn't really want to go home, and my mother let me stay with Daphne and her grandfather. The only condition was that Marcus was to go home for the night. I was happy not to go back to that place. It seemed as though it was an empty cavern of hate and pain. I still couldn't explain any of it. Daphne's grandfather looked at my left arm and the wounds that were there. He dipped the gauze in some liquid concoction that he made, and Marcus dressed the wounds.

I stared at the crown of Marcus's head as he spoke to me. "Amanda, did you do this to yourself?"

"No," I whispered back, not thinking he had heard me. He looked up. "I believe you."

Grandfather Shikoba said something in his native tongue, and Daphne responded, stood up, and sat beside me, watching me intently.

"Grandfather said that this will make the ache in your arms subside," Daphne stated out loud as he handed me a drink.

"What is it?" I asked, making a face.

"Boneset tea," Grandfather answered.

Grandfather Shikoba began to speak again. He then stood up and placed his open hand on my head. He then waved his hands back and forth.

It was Marcus's turn to speak. "Aki wants you to know about the land you live on. Do you believe in the human spirit?" he asked in seriousness.

I shook my head from side to side. "Human spirit?"

Grandfather spoke and Marcus translated, "Sometimes a spirit does not cross over and is lost, misguided, or not finished with something in this life. Sometimes when something terrible or unimaginable happens, it leaves an imprint. If someone had a violent ending or something tragic occurred, this will leave an aura of negativity."

Grandfather Shikoba walked over to a tall cabinet and pulled something from it that was wrapped in rawhide. He pulled out a sculpture of a small bear. "*Nitta Wosen*," Grandfather said.

"The bear," Marcus iterated. "This is a fetish."

The bear was made from turquoise. The light blue-green colors moved in their own pattern. It was small and fit in the palm of Grandfather Shikoba's hand. "A fetish is an old heirloom that has been passed down from generations. There is only one like it for a family unit. They are like amulets. This sacred piece can not only summon the spirits, but also take powers from entities."

I looked up at the Shikobas in shock. Had everyone gone mad? I just nodded and listened to Marcus.

Marcus shook his head as his grandfather spoke. I could tell he didn't want to tell me what his grandfather was saying, but after much persistence, Grandfather had gotten his way.

"Has anyone told you about the house your mother bought?"

I nodded slowly. "Daphne told me a bit about its history. I know that a lot of people that lived there have died or gone missing."

"Aki says that there is a story that is written on the walls of the caves about the land you live on." Grandfather continued to speak and Marcus translated, "It is a legend about a tribe that lived in that area. They were called the Penobscot. A medicine woman named Nita found a bear in the woods trapped in a pit and dying. Even though she feared the animal, she could not forgive herself if she left the creature to die slowly. She felt she had to save the bear, for she was named after the bear. Nita was saved by such a beast from the wilderness and brought to the tribe when she was an infant. With all the courage she could muster, she climbed into the hole and removed the wooden stake that was imbedded in its back. She was surprised to find that this creature was no ordinary animal. The beast had changed, and the bear became a man. She had saved the life of this creature and gained his favor. He promised her his protection and gave her his trust. The bear/man was a *witiko*."

I continued to listen to Grandfather's tale. "The witiko were originally human. If a man consumes human flesh, the witiko can possess them. When a witiko is changed to man and not in its true form, it is vulnerable and can easily die. The witiko had told her his secret in return for saving its life."

Marcus turned from his grandfather's direction and stared at me as he continued to translate. "Nita had heard the stories of these creatures and feared for her people. She asked him to change into an oak tree to hide. When he refused this request, she dared the witiko, saying he couldn't change into a tree. He did so, still in gratitude of Nita's deed to him. When he altered his form, the witiko didn't realize that he was on sacred ground. Only sacred ground can hold a spirit. Once bound in this form, he would remain until Nita chose to free him. It was said that Nita could summon it at anytime when she needed to, by spilling her own blood on the tree. Before the pale ones came, there was a siege on that land. Nita's people knew about the powerful spirit that was trapped deep inside the oak tree. The people begged her to release the witiko from its prison to save them. She refused to release it. She knew that once the creature was released, that its need for human flesh would consume it, and it would destroy the very people she wanted to protect. Out of desperation, her people sacrificed her in hopes to awaken him. She became the blood offering to draw the creature out of the bark. What the villagers didn't realize was that the witiko, whose name was Ahote, secretly loved Nita. That was how he became trapped in the pit. He had watched her for years and had saved her from the wilderness all those years before. He awakened from his sleep to find Nita dead and betrayed by her people. His vengeful spirit took over. He killed the invaders as the villagers had hoped, and then he turned on the whole nation in revenge. No one was spared. Innocent blood was spilled there. This desecrated the sacred land."

I then heard Grandfather Shikoba say, "*Shilup Chitoh Osh* ."

Marcus continued, "When this happened, the Great Spirit awoke from his slumber to see the massacre before him. He loved his brother and could not destroy him, so he bound him back in the tree and in the earth that he tainted. And as punishment, the dead are kept there to haunt him for all eternity. It is said that the evil spirit of Ahote still roams that land. He lurks in the woods and waits. He can turn into anything, blending like a chameleon. He cannot control his cravings. The anger and hate still resides there. Without blood or flesh, he cannot take form. When it is offered to him, he roams the land, but only for a short time. When he kills his victims, he takes in their energy. By doing this, he can stay longer."

I stared at the family in shock and doubt. It sounded just like the story of the boogeyman. But how could I explain the things I have seen in that house? Had I lost my mind?

"*Aiokpulo*," was the last word Grandfather said.

"It is evil," Marcus translated.

"Everyone loves, even malevolence," Grandfather said in perfect English.

"And do you think that's what attacked me?"

"No," Grandfather said. "It is the lost souls that the witiko controls that do this." Grandfather touched my arms for effect. "You are not crazy in the mind," Grandfather said and tapped the side of his head. "It's real. Witiko cannot come to you. The dead will bring you to him. "

Marcus held my hand tightly.

"It sees you," Grandfather said.

"Why me?"

"*Nanpisa*," Grandfather whispered as he pointed to his eyes.

"You are the one who sees them," Marcus interpreted.

Grandfather continued, "It will turn on your family now because you are not there." Grandfather moved closer in my direction. "It wants you, Haloka. You have an inner strength that radiates. It feels it," Grandfather pounded his chest. "It craves it." He placed the bear in my hands.

"This is your protector," Marcus told me.

Grandfather continued. "I felt it first day you came, Amanda. You are different. You and I are the same." Grandfather pointed to himself and then to me. "It sees you, and it knows you can see it."

"I don't know what to believe anymore," I said, afraid to believe it.

"If Grandfather says it's true, then it must be," Daphne said confidently.

I sat there in contemplation, wondering if all this was real or just a nightmare. I could hear the wind outside as it spoke its own language that only it could understand. I continued to ponder the possibilities. Was there the slightest chance that all this could be true? Logically the answer would be no, but I had seen so many things that not even I could explain. I worried about my family. How long would the house wait until it attacked them? I didn't want to wait to find that out. I looked up into Marcus's blue eyes. "What do I have to do?"

"We must awaken the Great Spirit and ask for his guidance," Grandfather replied, nodding his head. "He will show us the way."

"Maybe I should go home." I stood up ready to leave.

Grandfather placed his hands on my shoulders and sat me back down. "Tomorrow. In the light of day, he cannot harm. Night is different. Do not worry. Your family will be safe tonight."

I sat on the porch of Grandfather Shikoba's home. I hugged myself tightly as I gazed at the stars above. Daphne stayed inside and gave me some time to myself. I listened to the wind and watched the swaying of the trees. I closed my eyes and inhaled deeply, loving nature. It was getting colder. It had been raining a lot. The remnants of leaves cascaded down from the trees above. The ground was covered in red maple leaves. It looked like a crimson blanket covering the earth, keeping her warm. It was the day before All Hallows' Eve, but it felt like winter. Still, the land that Grandfather Shikoba lived on was beautiful.

I tried to make sense of all that was happening to me. Was I different or just crazy? My arms began to burn slightly, still sore from the incident. Did I do this to myself? I wanted to believe Grandfather Shikoba, but how can you believe the unbelievable? I was distracted from my thoughts and turned quickly when I heard the sound of the door hinges open and close. Marcus came up behind me and wrapped his arms around me. We stood in silence and watched the scene before us. He placed his chin on my head and sighed. I shivered and he brought me closer into his warm embrace, tightening his grip.

"Cold?" he asked in a hoarse tone.

"A little," I responded quickly. I turned to him and looked into his eyes. "Maybe I should go."

He held me tighter and shook his head, bringing his

face closer to mine. "Stay."

His eyes were begging me to stay. It pained me to say. "I think I have caused your family enough trouble as it is."

He smiled weakly. "If you haven't heard," he whispered, "I like trouble."

I started to speak, but he silenced me with one finger on my bottom lip. I closed my eyes as he tipped my chin up slightly. "I am here, Amanda. I am not going anywhere."

I became teary eyed, filled with confusion and fear. I nodded in agreement.

Marcus cupped my face with both of his palms and wiped the tears from my eyes with his thumbs. He moved closer. "What can I do?" he asked, gazing deeply into my eyes. "Is there anything I can do?"

He was so close. "Kiss me," I said.

He hesitated, surprised by my request, but quickly recovered. He dipped his head down and brushed his lips to mine in a slow motion. That's how it began, slowly and softly. His hands disappeared into my hair, bringing me closer to him. The kiss was indescribable; I could feel the raw power of it. I didn't know that one could become so lost in something as simple as a kiss. Yet this didn't seem so simple. I moved closer, mimicking his movements. I felt my back graze against the railing, but it didn't hurt. I became lost in the kiss. It was thrilling and scary at the same time. I wanted and needed Marcus more than anything. We stopped when we heard the door open. We moved apart slightly, but Marcus kept his hold on me. He smiled and slowly rubbed the side of my cheek with the back of his hand.

"Marcus," Grandfather whispered and then continued to speak in Choctaw.

Marcus nodded in agreement and looked at me once more. "I have to go." He let go, and once again I was alone.

Chapter 15

Arriving home early in the morning was hard. It was the first time I had been there since that night. Marcus took me home. As the motorcycle approached the gates on Water Street, I could feel a twinge of fear. Marcus must have known by the change in pressure of my grip. Marcus rubbed my hands lightly as he stood up, forcing me to let him go so he could get off the bike. "It's all right, Amanda. It's like Aki said. During daylight, you're safe."

Marcus walked over to the gates and pushed them open. "Do you want me to drive you to the house?"

I thought about it, but I knew that if my mother saw Marcus she would immediately think that we had been together all night. The truth was he did leave and came back in the morning as promised. I didn't want any complications today. I shook my head no. "Sorry."

Marcus smiled knowingly. "It's okay. I understand."

I slung my backpack on my shoulder as I stood up from the bike. Marcus placed the carving of the bear in my hands and closed my fingers over it. His hands lingered over mine as he stared up at me. "You'll call me, right, if you need me?"

I nodded in agreement as I dipped my head down

toward his. I looked at him eye to eye as I stole a kiss. I knew it was a bold move. He didn't move away. He accepted it, taking in all that I had to give and giving in return. I opened my eyes when he ended it. He stared at me, giving a smile of approval. We kissed again, but this time it was his doing. It didn't last as long as the other night, but it was at least something. He then kissed my forehead like I was a child.

"Do you want me to come over later?" he asked concerned.

"Yes, definitely." No other words were said. Marcus started the bike. I couldn't help myself; I had to hold him again, hugging him tightly before he left. He made a noise that sounded like a laugh when he turned the motor off and got off the motorcycle. He held me as I listened to the rhythm of his heart. Marcus was much taller than me. I was only five and a half feet tall. Marcus was taller. It felt like we were made for each other. It was the one moment that I wished time would stop or at least slow down a bit. It seemed this was the only peace that I had left. He took the cold away and replaced it with warmth within me. It was then that I felt completely safe. I heard his sigh as he let me go. His leather jacket groaned as he released me from his embrace.

"I have to go." His hand lingered on my chin as he tipped up head upwards toward his face.

"I know," was all I could say.

"I'll be back."

"You better be."

He sealed his pledge with another kiss. A long, deep, passionate kiss, assuring me that he would return soon. At that time nothing else mattered.

"Bye," he said after he broke the kiss. He winked at me as he hopped back on his bike. He turned one last time and then drove off. I held the carving in my hand and whispered a brief prayer to myself as I walked up the pathway to the house, not getting the warm welcome I had hoped for. I stood before the front door of 210 Water Street still holding the only means of protection in my hands. With heavy feet, I walked in.

Upon entering, all I heard was the sound of my mother's voice shouting at someone. Instinctively I ran to the sound of her voice to find out what was wrong. I found my mother in the living room with an elderly woman. The strange woman sipped out of her coffee cup while my mother was ranting. The woman was serenely calm. "Hello, Amanda," the woman said without turning around. "I have been waiting for you."

"Ah … hi," was all I could say in return. When the woman finally looked in my direction, I recognized her. It was the woman standing outside the doctor's office the other day. Her brown eyes stared deeply into mine.

"Amanda, please go upstairs." My mother rubbed her face in her hands as she said this.

When I hesitated, she was more persistent. "Amanda, now!"

I slowly began walking to the staircase, trying to listen to every word, but all I did hear was a lot of mumbling. There was only a word or two that I could make out. I knew that I had seen her yesterday, but I knew I had seen her somewhere else. But where?

Lauren kept her arms crossed. "What do you want, Ivy?"

Ivy inhaled and then exhaled slowly. She placed her teacup down and stood up. "What do I want? What do I want? Well, let's start off with what any grandparent wants, and that's to see her kin before she dies."

"I thought I made myself perfectly clear eleven years ago, Ivy. Nothing has changed."

"Do you hate me that much that you would deny me seeing my kin?"

"I have never approved of the things that your family does. I do not want to subject Amanda to that nonsense." Lauren waved her arms across herself like an umpire showing her displeasure.

"Whether you approve of my talents or not isn't my concern. What needs to be addressed is the fact that Amanda, whether you like it or not, has a gift and needs to be told."

"I will not have you fill my daughter's head with your lies."

"Is that what you really believe? I thought after the years you spent with Lucas you would see the truth."

"All I saw was that my husband was delusional and needed help. You only made things worse by encouraging him. Lucas was sick."

Ivy couldn't control herself any longer. "Is that what you thought? Lucas wasn't sick, and you know it. It just scared you. It is you who is delusional. Your ignorance is going to cost you, Lauren. Do you want to endanger your daughter as well? Amanda needs to know the truth."

"And what truth is that, Ivy? Your truth? She has no clue about her father's illness, and I have no intentions of telling her."

Ivy lowered her head in defeat. She knew Lauren wouldn't budge today. "Okay, Lauren. You win for now. I will honor your request." Ivy looked up in Lauren's direction. "This house isn't good. It doesn't like the fact that I am present. I will leave, but it's only because the negative energy doesn't want me here." Ivy rubbed her arms for warmth. "All I ask is to see my kin. You don't have to say who I am. All I want to do is look at her."

Ivy held her head in her hands and looked up once more at Lauren. "Lauren, your mam wanted me to tell you she loves you, and you need to leave this house. She has been talking continuously since I arrived."

Lauren was quiet and trying to maintain her composure.

Ivy continued, "She also says that there is a piece of property at home that was overlooked, and you should contact Jim Morris, her solicitor."

Lauren crossed her arms in disbelief. "No talk of ghosts; I mean it."

Ivy interrupted her. "She's not a ghost, Lauren. She's crossed over. Your mam just likes to visit once in a while." Ivy stopped for a moment like she was listening to someone. "She says you've done a fine job and is surprised that you've kept your velveteen rabbit. She said, 'Bunny, I am proud of the woman you've become.'"

Lauren's jaw dropped, and then the rage took over. "How dare you? How dare you?" Lauren pointed toward the door for effect. "GET OUT."

Ivy's grin subsided. "Lauren."

"GET OUT!" she screamed at the top of her lungs.

"Please let me see my——"

"GET OUT!" Lauren shouted, interrupting Ivy and pointing her finger toward the front door.

Ivy looked behind Lauren. "I told you that would make things worse for me, Ness. Thanks for all the bloody help." Her big bracelets jingled as she raised her hands, pointing behind Lauren. "Go back to the light. That's the last time I speak for you."

Ivy then directed her gaze at Lauren. "I will be in town at the motel if you change your mind." Ivy looked around the house in disgust. "This place has a horrible history, Lauren. It is a place of hate, sorrow, and blood." Ivy held her head in her hands like she was in pain. "I can smell the blood."

"Don't worry, Ivy. We will be gone soon enough." With that, Ivy let herself out and Lauren slammed the door behind her.

Lauren started to weep when she heard the door close. It was the first time in fourteen years she had cried over her mother. She wiped the tears from her face. "Damn you, Ivy." Lauren walked up two flights of stairs and then walked to the trapdoor of the attic. She pulled down the stairs and ascended into the attic. As she turned on the light, the hollow room echoed with sound. Every step she took made her heart fill with grief.

Lauren wiped her face again and walked over to the trunk below the arched window. The wind startled her a bit when she heard the tree branch hit the pane. It was like a sign from nature, warning her of dredging up the past. The small branch screeched against the glass as Lauren knelt before the chest. The mahogany pine box still had its smell. The old fashioned lock reflected the light from the room and twinkled. She pulled out her necklace that held a key along with a locket. She removed the chain from her neck and stared at it. She slowly placed the key in the lock of the trunk and turned it. The click of the catch made her stop and linger for a moment. With a small sigh and closed eyes, she opened the lid of the trunk. A lot of the objects were covered with fabric. One that was covered with a piece of emerald green satin caught her eye. She slowly removed the covered object, being careful not to drop it. When the cloth was removed, she rubbed her hands against the fabric of the old toy. She held it up to the light to view a velveteen rabbit. Its lifeless eyes looked out at her with its curious stare. "Damn you, Ivy. Damn you." The tears fell again. She delved deeply into the box and found a music box. She caressed the heart shaped lid as she opened it. She lingered, looking into the small mirror that was attached to the inside of the lid. As she gazed at her reflection, she spoke out loud, "I miss you, Lucas. I wish you were here. I don't know what to do. Please tell me what to do."

Lauren held the rabbit and hugged it tightly to her chest. She kneeled there in silence, waiting for an answer that would never come. Mom didn't know I was there, watching her. I didn't know who the woman was, but she seemed to have a great effect on my mother. She jumped when she heard my voice from behind her. "Mom, have you seen Taboo? I haven't seen her since I came home."

She continued to wipe her face quickly before she stood up. "Amanda," she said regaining her composure. "I didn't hear you come up."

"Are you okay?" was all I could ask.

Mom waved the rabbit from side to side a bit so I could see it and brought the object down in the cradle of her arms. "Just thinking of my mother. That's all."

I walked closer, and she closed the trunk. She still held the rabbit.

"Grandma gave you that?" I asked.

"Yes. Where I lived, we call grandmothers, nanny. When I was a little girl, I was sick. The doctors said that I had tuberculosis. A lot of people back then contracted it. I was fortunate; many children died. I survived because the doctors found a cure. My mam used to read me the story about a velveteen rabbit." Lauren laughed. "She even called me Bunny. My mam found the story comforting. It gave her hope through those scary times."

Mom caressed the stuffed animal. With loving care, she handed it over to me so I could get a closer look.

"It's soft." Its cold doll eyes looked out without a care. I moved its ears from side to side in hopes of getting a smile from Mom's lips. It worked, but only for a short time. I handed it back to her, and she turned to the chest again.

She opened the lid of the chest again and removed the heart shaped music box she had held earlier. When she opened it, it played a familiar tune. I stood still. "What song is that?"

Mom laughed. "Do you like it? It's called "Camelot." Your father bought it for me the day you were born."

I gave Mom a distressed look. "What's inside the box, Mom?" I walked over to take a better look, trying to peer over her shoulders.

She pulled it from my view, "Why?"

"It looks familiar, that's all."

"I can't see how it would be familiar. It's been in this trunk for many years, love."

I could see the writing on the lid. "With all my love forever, Lucas" was etched on it. Mom finally opened it again and turned it in my direction. The red velvet lining inside contained many clippings of newspaper articles. Then I saw it, a slight glare of light that reflected off a small silver object in the box. When I tried to touch it, she shut the lid quickly. "It's just some news articles, that's all, Penn." My mother called me Penn sometimes. It was the nickname she gave me a long time ago.

"Of what?"

Mom rubbed the top of the box gently and said, "They're about your dad."

"Really?" I asked, excited. "Can I see them?"

"Amanda, there are some things that you don't know about your dad, and I don't expect you to understand."

I didn't like where this conversation was going. "Understand what? Does this have anything to do with that woman that was here? Who was she?"

Lauren couldn't hide the truth any longer. She hoped that I would forgive her one day. "That woman is from my country." She took her hand in mine. "She's your dad's nanny, Amanda."

I pulled my hand away quickly. "But you said——"

"I know what I said." Mom moved closer to me.

I stepped back.

"I was only looking out for you. That's all."

"Why are you telling me this now?"

Mom laughed sarcastically. She moved her hand across her face, removing the small strands of hair that were in her eyes. "I don't know. I really don't know. She wants to see you. I don't want her to, but you are old enough to decide that for yourself."

"Mom," I asked with an outstretched hand, "what did this woman do that was so wrong that you don't want me to see her?"

"It's not what she did, Amanda. It's what she is."

I stared at my mother, confused.

"Your father grew up in a traveling caravan of gypsies, acrobats, magicians, and others of different talents. You are gypsy, Amanda, from your father's side."

I listened intently to her story.

"The gypsies were supposedly the last survivors of the last Egyptian dynasty. The remaining line immigrated to Europe. They used to come around to the village when I was a child with little paper flowers to sell. They were the ugliest things I ever saw." Mom laughed out loud, remembering the past. Knowing full well she was rambling on, she went back on the topic of my father.

"It was when I was sixteen that I met your father. The caravans came through like they always did in September. I felt adventurous and went to their festival that they always held to bring in a pence or two. I went with a few of my mates. There I saw him. He was in the show with Ivy."

Mom briefly closed her eyes, remembering more of the yesterdays. "Your father never knew his father or his mother. Ivy's son was your dad's father. He died before Lucas was born. Lucas's mother died giving birth to him. Ivy is actually your great nanny. He always called her Mum."

Toby had heard all the commotion and walked in while we were talking.

"Dad was in the circus?" I asked curiously.

Mom remained silent, trying to find the right words for what she was about to say. She chose her words carefully, fearing that she might inadvertently say the wrong thing. "This was no ordinary circus." She decided to quickly let it spill from her mouth to get it over quickly. "Your father claimed that he could see things other people couldn't see. He said he could see people who passed on."

"What?" Toby and I asked in unison.

"Your dad was sick. Your nanny didn't help the situation. She encouraged him, saying that she could see them too. In the beginning I thought he realized it was an act and played the role. I never knew until later that he truly believed it."

"You mean dad was like a ghost consultant?" Toby asked.

I asked, "Why, after all this time, would Nanny come here?"

Mom held her head down. "Your Great Nanny says she doesn't like the house. Don't worry about it. She's just an old woman that wants to see her family. I am sorry I didn't tell you sooner. I had hoped she would never find us." Mom looked at me, waiting for something. "She seems eager to see you, Amanda."

"And why would that be?" I asked.

"I think we both know why."

Toby threw his hands up in the air in defeat and walked down the attic stairs.

Mom started by saying, "All I ask is that if you do choose to speak with her, don't listen to her crazy stories. I don't want you to become wrapped up in her fantasy. She may sound convincing, but it's not real."

"I can't believe you never said anything about this. Especially with everything that's been going on. I may be sick like Dad, and you never once said anything this whole time!"

"Amanda you're not sick."

"How do you know?"

"I think I know my daughter."

"Do you know what people say about this house?"

Mom didn't say a word.

"I have heard a lot of stories lately."

"I didn't know until recently, Amanda. I swear to that. That's why we are leaving."

"This house has a very gruesome history, Mom. That's

why people don't come here, and that's why it's never been sold."

"It's just a house, Amanda. A house," she shouted. Lauren tried to calm down. "People create their own lives and hardships. Houses have nothing to do with it." Mom waved her arms for effect. "Houses do not live or breathe. They do not have a pulse, and they especially don't attack young girls in the middle of the night."

I started to walk away.

"Amanda, I am sorry honey, please don't..."

I didn't hear another word she had to say to me after that. I decided to shut her out. I know Mom was scared and angry, but so was I. I pulled the bear carving out of my pocket and gripped it tightly. It was time to find out who Nanny Pennington really was. Crazy or not, wasn't she family? If Grandfather Shikoba says there's more going on than meets the eye, then I am a believer. Besides, it's some kind of answer to the things that are going on here. Toby was standing right in my way as I walked to the door to leave.

"Are you going to find her?"

"I guess that's what I am doing, yes."

Toby's eyes twinkled with excitement. "I am going with you."

I tried to stop him. "Toby, you are grounded, remember?"

"That's okay. I'll deal with Mom later." He shrugged.

Besides, what kind of brother would I be to let you go off on your own?"

We ran out the door while Mom was shouting my name.

Lauren still knelt before the big trunk and pulled out the pairs of baby booties that lay next to the music box. As she knelt down, she caressed the soft fabric and then collapsed to the floor in grief again. She held the cordless phone in her hand and decided to make a call. "Jim Morris, please."

As Lauren waited patiently on hold, she caressed the little pairs of shoes again. She pulled out a picture from the jewelry box and held it to her breast. She didn't expect to find a picture that she hadn't seen in sixteen years. The grief within became more intense. She wiped her tears and lovingly touched the photo. All she could think about was Amanda and setting things right. She sat in deep thought as she waited for Jim Morris. When Amanda came back, they would talk more. Lauren left the attic and then began to pack.

Chapter 16

Ivy walked on the grounds looking for a source. As she held out her hands, she could feel the energy pulling her toward it. She walked over to a small clearing and observed a small glen. She frowned slightly as she felt the intensity of energy. She needed to know what she was dealing with. Ivy took her brown sandals off and placed them on the ground before reaching the glen as a sign of respect. As she moved out into the clearing, she felt the sheer burning sensation on her bare feet. The ground was not sacred at all; it was tainted. She could feel the vortex taking her in, pulling her into the unknown past. She could hear their screams and she could feel their pain. She was drawn to the large oak that ominously posed still and silent. It was old and hollow. All that was left was the outer shell. She grabbed a piece of the bark and pulled it downward. She heard a distant moaning sound as some sap ran from the fresh wound. Ivy touched it and rubbed the sticky substance between her fingers. She inhaled its fragrance. The large tree was different; Ivy didn't know why. It just seemed out of place. She touched it and jerked back quickly. Her heart increased its tempo. "Oh, my," she quickly said breathlessly. The echoes of the voices from the distant past called to her.

As she inhaled deeply, she could see her mother's look of disapproval and fear. "It's just a quick peek, mam. I'll be in and out before you know it." Ivy's mother didn't approve, but Ivy still took the risk. She caressed the texture of the bark, and she felt her heart drop as she was moved into another plane. When she felt the ground beneath stabilize, she opened her eyes to gain some insight into the past. All that greeted her were a pair of eyes looking back at her. It looked like a native woman from some tribe. Her deerskin clothing and moccasins were blood stained and dirty. She shook her head side to side in a look of panic. Ivy tried to break the language barrier.

"Are you lost?" Ivy asked, in hopes to help her move on into the light.

The woman refused to move. It seemed as she was warning her of the dangers within. The skies above turned red and dark purple with an orange contrast. The wind started to gust downward into the clearing. Lightning bolts thrust themselves into the ground close to where Ivy stood. The ground trembled with such force that it knocked Ivy from her feet. "Bugger," she shouted as she tried to regain her stance. "I am getting too old for this."

The woman tried to help her up as the plane became more unstable. Ivy was not welcome. She never was, but that never stopped her from forcing an entry into the unknown. A large mist-like structure started to form in the distance. Ivy's white hair came undone from its tight bun and cascaded down. The wind forced itself against her body and her hair whipped wildly across her face. She couldn't see. "Damn." She moved her hair quickly to see what was coming. "I can help you," Ivy shouted, but the woman again refused and pushed Ivy to the side as the ground opened up. Ivy could hear a sound coming from the hole below. The strange woman started to chant and shout. Ivy looked into the pit in horror.

Other souls started to crawl from the void. They remained in appearance as they died in life. Their cries were inaudible to Ivy's ears, but the other woman understood them well. They looked like souls of the damned. Their frightened faces continued to pour out, running from something. All ceased when a grumbling began from below. The ground moved up and down like it was breathing. It was as though the ground had a life of its own.

Something was coming from underground, wanting to show itself to Ivy. She held her hands to her eyes to block the light. She wanted to know what it was that haunted this land and tormented these souls. Large antlers were the first characteristic to appear. The more that came into view, the more frightened Ivy became. The face and body were covered in hair like a wolf. Its hands were like talons from a bird. Its fingernails were long and pointed. Its yellow teeth were jagged and long. It appeared like it was smiling at her. There was no nose or lips visible, just teeth. Its legs were shaped like dog legs. As it continued to climb from below, a clouded mist appeared around the creature. The lost souls disappeared, and the beast was no longer a beast but a man.

"What do you want here?" Ivy asked as the man came closer.

He didn't look happy but strode forward with a purpose. As he spoke the voice sounded distorted and deep. He was talking so quickly that Ivy could not keep up. She wished she could understand. The scenery was crumbling around her, leaving nothing but blackness. Ivy tried to move back to the present, knowing full well she overstepped herself this time. The ground shook again, and she fell hard this time. Ivy raised her hand to ward him off, for she didn't have the energy to go back as she came. Before he could touch her, the other woman touched him, holding him steadfast. He didn't move, He was stunned by the woman's touch. She turned to Ivy once more and uttered one word. "*Kucha* (Out)!"

There was an explosion that pushed Ivy backwards, back to her normal plane. She lay flat on her back stunned by the magnitude of this thing's energy. She finally had enough strength to push her body up into a sitting position. As she gazed at the tree, her thoughts ran in a hundred directions. "Oh, my."

Lauren didn't know where else to go. She didn't know very many people. She sat in her car staring at the sign for the law firm that Trent Shikoba owned. She saw that the light was still on in his office, but she didn't know what else to do. She knew that Amanda was fond of Marcus and thought that maybe Trent had some idea of her whereabouts. She didn't want to contact the police yet. Amanda wasn't gone long enough for Lauren to start panicking. Her hopes faded as she saw the lights go out. Lauren began to get out of the car when she saw Trent walk outside and turn to lock the door. She didn't know why she came, but she needed to talk to someone. Wasn't a lawyer the best answer?

"Mr. Shikoba," she yelled as she breathlessly ran to him.

Trent tried to adjust his focus in the darkness to see who was coming his way. His expression changed into a slight smile when he saw Lauren. It disappeared when he noticed her distress. Trent looked down at his watch to look at the time. "Ms. Pennington, what are you doing out here at this hour?"

Lauren was next to him. Trent waited for her to catch her breath. "I know it is late, and I am sorry," she stumbled out. "This is a bit awkward for me." She waited a moment to find the right words. "I was wondering if you had seen Amanda today."

The hairs on the back of his neck rose. "I am sorry, Ms. Pennington. Can't say that I have."

Lauren wrung her hands together, not knowing what to do next. "She's not answering the phone. Amanda and I had a bit of a tiff this afternoon. She left angry. I thought that maybe Marcus or Daphne had seen her."

Trent shook his head. "Daphne is at her grandfather's, and Marcus was working late today. He did mention that he was going to stop over at your house this evening." Trent turned the lock to open the door again. "Why don't you come in? You look cold."

"Still not used to the weather, I am afraid," she said with chattering teeth. "Yes, thank you, if you don't mind."

Trent directed his arm out toward the hallway.

"Thanks again. It's just that I don't know many people around here, and after our conversation, I was hoping you wouldn't mind." She stopped when she started to ramble.

Trent watched her stumble with her words. "Would you like to sit down?" he asked as he pointed to a chair.

Lauren looked around and spotted the chair. "Thank you," she said, still shivering. She sat down, rubbing her hands together. "I am afraid I made an error in judgment. Her grandmother came to the house today." She looked at Trent. "I have been keeping her from Amanda. There was a bit of bad blood between us, you could say." Lauren rubbed her hands again in attempt to gain some warmth. "I don't know what else to do," she whispered in desperation. "I am starting to question if it was a good idea to move here."

Trent moved closer to Lauren and bent down before

her. "Lauren, there is no book on parenting. Believe me, I have made my mistakes. Still do," he stated as a matter of fact. "I wouldn't worry too much. I am sure she's probably home right now waiting for you. She's a good kid."

Lauren laughed sarcastically. "You don't even know Amanda."

"I have seen enough changes in Marcus to say that Amanda is good for him. He's become a better man."

Lauren didn't look comforted.

"I will call Daphne to see if she's talked to Amanda, if it will ease your mind."

Lauren just nodded with her head bowed down. She didn't want to cry. "I appreciate it, Mr. Shikoba."

"Please call me Trent."

Lauren raised her head and finally looked around Trent's legal office. She could smell the pine shelves. There were papers scattered across the large desk before her. The carpet was a shade of burgundy. All the dark colors made the room gloomy. She could see old Chinese food, still in their containers, lined up against the window sill. She thought she saw an old pizza box in the corner of the room. To the far right of the room, there was a small bar with decanters filled with different types of liquor.

"Would you like something to drink?" Trent asked.

Lauren nodded her head. "Water, please."

He smiled as he walked up to the small refrigerator in the back of the room. His brown eyes made contact with

Lauren's as she took a deep drink.

"Better?"

Lauren nodded again.

He stuck his hands in his pockets, trying to retrieve his phone. "Excuse me for a moment, Lauren." He took the phone from his pocket as he walked from the room, closing the door.

Lauren wanted to get up and eavesdrop on the conversation, but she thought better of it. He wasn't gone long. When he returned to the room, he told Lauren that Daphne had not seen Amanda since early this morning.

Lauren stood up. "Thank you, Trent. Sorry about keeping you this evening."

"Not a problem. I am sure that she's home by now."

"For some reason I don't think so, but thanks anyway." Lauren rubbed her temples, praying for inner peace. She didn't want to burden Trent any longer, so she changed the subject. "I called my mother's solicitor today." Lauren hesitated before she continued. "He told me today that there was a piece of property that Mam left me. It was overlooked somehow. When I called and asked him about it, he was, needless to say, a bit embarrassed."

"And how did you learn of the news?" Trent asked curiously.

Lauren placed her cup down on the table and stood up, "You wouldn't believe me if I told you. To be honest, I don't believe it myself."

When she turned to leave, Trent called out for her attention again. "Ms. Pennington, if there's anything I can do for you, call me."

Lauren thought on that a moment. "You know, Mr. Shikoba, I actually do have a favor to ask of you." She looked up at him square in the eye. "What can you tell me about the house I live in?"

Chapter 17

Toby and I took a bus to the center of town. It was the strangest thing. Toby knew where to find Ivy. We stared at the neon sign that said Jet Stream Hotel.

"Are you sure she's here?"

"She has to be. The guy at the main desk said she booked a room here."

We walked over and stood before the room with the number seven. I turned in his direction. "How did you know she was here?"

Toby smirked. "Amanda, it's the only motel in this city."

"Oh," I responded in surprise. I hesitated to knock on the door. "This feels wrong, Toby. Maybe we should wait."

"Wait? Wait for what? Just knock on the door, Amanda."

"I just feel bad going behind Mom's back."

"I am sure Mom will understand. We want to know Ivy. She'll get over it in time."

I started to regret my hasty decision in coming. This wasn't the way. When I thought longer about it, I had second thoughts. I backed away from the door.

"Amanda Pennington, are you a scaredy cat?"

"No, I am not."

Toby laughed. "I thought you weren't scared of

anything, big sis."

"Don't call me that. I am only five minutes older than you, butthead."

When I slapped him, I heard a woman's voice call my name. I turned to see the woman that we were looking for standing by a flight of stairs. I didn't respond. I just glared.

"It is you, Amanda. You look so much like your father." She smiled as she greeted me.

I turned to my side. "This is my brother, Toby."

Ivy stopped in her tracks for a second and tilted her head to one side. "Toby?" she asked.

"My brother. You knew I had a brother, right?"

Ivy quickly recovered. "Yes, I did know you had a brother." She moved closer to look at us. I figured her vision was fading in her years. She looked beside me and smiled. "Hello, Toby. I am your great-nanny Ivy."

Toby smiled in return.

"Who's the other lady with you?" I asked, looking at the woman in an old yellow cotton dress.

"This is my Mam."

I was taken aback by her answer. "How old is she?"

The woman behind Ivy laughed out loud. "I am very, very old, lassie."

"Please, Mam, not now." Ivy ushered Toby and me inside her room. "Come inside now. I need to speak to you."

It was an awkward moment, but after all, she was

family. My father was ill, and I needed to know more about him. I decided to start the conversation, "My Mom didn't want us to come, but Toby and I thought it would be a good idea to see you. You did travel all this way to see us."

Ivy just stared at me in wonder. "I can't believe how much you look like your dad."

I just smiled in return. "I wanted to ask you some questions about him, if you don't mind."

Ivy smoothed her dress with her hands as she sat down. "What is it you want to know?"

I figured I would just be blunt. "Was he crazy?"

Nanny Ivy began to laugh. She couldn't help it. I supposed she found my directness humorous.

"CRAZY? Lucas? Never. He was such a dear." She wiped the tears from her eyes because she was laughing so hard. "Lucas was a lot better at sight than I was. He was a wonderful man."

"All right. Then what was wrong with him?"

"I am surprised you're asking me that question, when you see them yourself."

"Excuse me?" I asked confused.

"The woman behind me, Amanda. The one I told you was me Mam."

I nodded.

"Amanda, my Mam is a hundred five years old."

I shrugged. "She looks good."

The woman laughed again behind Nanny Ivy. "I love

that grandchild of mine. She is such a warm soul. Isn't she, Ivy?"

"Yes, Mam, she is that." She waited, for what I didn't know. She looked confused. "This is going to be harder than I thought." She moved closer to me. "Amanda, my Mam is dead."

I didn't know what to say to that. I was very perplexed.

"Okay, forget that. Tell me about the strange things that have happened to you in your life."

I was very quiet.

"Did you find yourself talking to people that others couldn't see?"

"I was a child," I finally responded. "Children have imaginary friends."

"Is that what society calls them today? Imaginary friends? I call them what they are. The dead need to speak. They try to reach out to the living for help. Just some of us are more sensitive than most."

Toby laughed.

"Okay, let's put it this way." Nanny stood up and started to move her hands around as she spoke out. "There are people today that can see auras. Science said they were a bunch of frauds. But now, years later, science has designed a computer that can see a person's aura. Now it is proven that auras exist, and they are looking more into it." She quickly plopped down beside me in excitement. "Don't you see? Just because science cannot prove it, doesn't mean it doesn't exist. They just haven't found a way to see it for themselves."

I still didn't say a word. I think she could sense that she was losing me.

"Some people can see more than three dimensions. There are other planes of life, Amanda. Different transitions. That cold chill some get or that feeling of being touched. Is it nerves and muscles, or is it a loved one trying to reach you?"

Oh no, Mom was right about her. I looked at her intently.

"When you get that intuition or vibe, is it you or something else?"

I had to get away. I stood up. "I shouldn't have come here. I am sorry to waste your time." I could tell that my response upset her.

"Sit down, please. Amanda, whether you like it or not, you have a gift. Accept it." She looked over to Toby. "Tell her, Toby."

Toby looked baffled himself. "Tell her what?"

"She needs to know, Toby. Please tell her."

Toby shook his head no.

"All right, then, I will." Ivy looked at me again. "When a person has the gift, a family member like my Mam stays to be that person's guide into the unknown. They help them in the transition." She hesitated briefly before she said, "Amanda, Toby is your guide."

"Excuse me?" I asked, confused.

"Amanda, Toby doesn't exist on this plane." Nanny Ivy held my hand. "He's dead."

I stood up in shock and in denial. "You're crazy."

Ivy stood up. "Ask your mother if you don't believe me, but I warn you, it will only upset her. Amanda, Toby died."

The room began to spin. I held my head tightly and tried to breathe. I could feel the darkness taking hold.

"Think back, Amanda. Has your mother ever spoken to Toby? Has she ever responded to his presence? Toby isn't alive. He has grown as an infant with you. You're twins, Amanda. Twins are very close, even in death."

"Please stop," Toby shouted. "Stop, you're hurting her."

"Tell her, Toby. She needs to know."

"All right," he shouted. "All right."

Tears welled up in my eyes as Toby looked at me. "Amanda, I didn't think you were ready for the truth."

"What are you talking about?" I screamed in frustration. "You have a room."

"It's a spare room that Mom always makes up. I thought that would make things easier."

"Our conversations together?"

Toby thought long and hard. "In the beginning it was easy. Like you said, Mom thought you had imaginary friends. As you've gotten older, Mom probably thought you were talking to the cat, yourself, or her."

"The fight with Nathan," I stated in desperation.

"It was someone else who was in the fight, Amanda. It was another new kid. I figured if I told you it was me, it would still make me real to you, and it would explain why Mom removed all those things from my room. I didn't think you were ready yet."

"The kids at the beach spoke to you."

"Did they? Or were they speaking to someone else?"

"I don't believe it. I can't."

Nanny Ivy sat close to me. She placed an arm around me in hopes of calming me. "You can't help it, love. To us they look real. It's not like the pictures show it. To us they are a solid form and alive."

"I am sure my mother had heard me say his name," I said, confident of that fact.

Ivy placed her hands in her lap and looked down. "No, Amanda. You gave him the name. Your brother was named after his father. She wouldn't have known who you were referring to." She nodded her head at me. "It was after that your mother broke ties with me. You father loved your mam. He did what he felt was best for her at the time, and that was to deny what he was. He went to doctors and took tablets. The tablets only intensified the manifestations."

I covered my face, still shaking my head. "How did he die?"

Toby looked at Ivy in warning. "It's too soon."

"Amanda, I think you've had enough of a shock for

today, kid."

"How did he die?" I shouted in anger.

Ivy's bottom lip quivered. "Maybe you should ask your mam that question."

"I am asking you. I need to know."

Ivy stood up and walked over to the window. "Regardless of what you think of me, we do believe in a higher power." She turned in my direction as she held a small cross that was attached to a chain around her neck. "I feared for your father, Amanda. He had done something that made him lost. His soul will forever wander."

I interrupted her. "What happened?"

"He died tragically," she stuttered with a tear in her eye. "The medication made his visions uncontrollable. It hurt. It was too much. A medium can have control, with practice. Drugs relax the mind and leave it open to outside influences. When people like us are in a drug-induced state, spirits can be dangerous for us. " Ivy put her head down. "He took his own life." She continued to stare out of the clear glass. "His only wish from me was to be buried at Highgate Cemetery with the rest of the family. I did what he asked of me."

I shook my head.

"The other side can take control, causing possessions and such. Your father feared that something would happen to you or your mother. He believed that you were in danger as long as he was with you." Ivy collapsed into a chair by the window. "He called me in a panicked state. It was the first time I had heard from him in five years. He told me he was sorry for what he had done to me and he loved me." Ivy looked down. "Then I heard a sound, and I knew he was gone." She placed her hands on top of her head in grief. "I have been looking for him ever since. He hadn't crossed over, and we do not believe in suicide. It's against our principles." She looked up at me again. "What scared him the most was he knew you were like us. I am so sorry, Amanda." Ivy reached out to take my hand again for comfort, and I moved away.

I walked over to the door and spoke, not turning around. "My whole life has been filled with secrets. Everything about me is a lie."

"Amanda, whether you believe it or not, the fact remains you are in danger."

I was going to go. "I saw it, Amanda," Ivy shouted. "I have never seen anything like it before. I don't believe this thing has ever lived. It is imperative that you and your mother leave that place as soon as possible."

"I need some air." I looked at Toby. "Are you coming?" I figured I would fix him for this game he concocted. Just before he could walk through the doorway, I slammed the door in front of him, trying to teach him a lesson. Then the unexpected happened.

He walked right through it.

Chapter 18

Cheryl Thornhope looked at the old house with a sneer. "I'll teach you to mess with me."

Cheryl was so angry she could spit. Jack wouldn't even come with her to defend her honor. He actually told Cheryl she deserved everything she got. She made a small sound, thinking back on her and Jack's argument. She couldn't believe the way things had been going for her this year. If truth be told, she was still upset about Marcus. Cheryl still had feelings for him. It hurt when he came home and didn't even bother to try to patch things up between them. She felt like they had chemistry. Cheryl always did the finishing. It stung her pride a bit that Marcus was the one who ended the relationship. To find him with that Pennington girl only made things worse. Cheryl rubbed her right cheek that was still bruised from Amanda's punch. "That little witch is going to get what she deserves."

Cheryl had big plans for Amanda tonight. She dragged the bag of goodies that she brought with her. She waited in the bushes, waiting for everyone to go to bed. Instead, she observed precious Amanda leaving, talking to herself. Even better, her mother left the house too. When she saw everyone leave the house, it made things more interesting.

She smiled in triumph. Cheryl had heard from some friends at school that Amanda was attacked by someone. She only wished she was there to see that. She looked down, jingling the bag. "This is going to be great."

Cheryl was supposed to wait for Amber, but she decided to start without her. *No time like the present*, she thought. Cheryl knew an opportunity when it showed itself. Cheryl walked toward the house, happy with her plan. She had a trick or two in that bag. She smiled wider when she thought about the rumors going around about Amanda seeing a shrink. Well, if that was the case, Amanda will sure need counseling after this night. As Cheryl approached the front the door, she found it odd that it was open, welcoming her entry. She could have sworn that it was closed a second before. With the mother leaving the house as quickly as she did, Cheryl assumed that she didn't close the door properly. She waited a moment, worried that maybe someone was still inside the house. She thought better about it and decided to shout out to see if she got a response. She waited, getting no answer in return.

Cheryl beamed with excitement. She couldn't wait to hear all the gossip at school come Monday morning. She had to settle the score between them. "After this, she'll never mess with me again," she stated with confidence.

When she was sure the coast was clear, she walked in and closed the door. The first thing that surprised her was how big the house actually was on the inside. She wanted to move quickly, not knowing when anyone would come back. She whistled gingerly as she moved throughout the house, trying to find Amanda's room. The place was so large Cheryl, hoped she didn't get lost. She took to the stairs hurriedly, now regretting that she had come inside. When she finally hit the top of the stairs, she made a quick right. Cheryl was a bit out of breath. The bag seemed heavier, the more she walked. Her forehead and palms began sweating as she plopped the bag down, finding what she hoped was the right room. She began by opening the balcony window by the window seat to get some air. Some trinket that was dangling fell to the floor. Cheryl left it there, not bothering to put it back into place. She knew she had to be quick, before someone saw her. She knelt down and rummaged in the black plastic bag. She spilled a bit of canola oil on the floor by the door in the bedroom. She then went toward the closet door. She pulled on the string that was hanging in front of her to turn the light on, so she could see. She bent down again and placed the mannequin with the noose around its neck on the bar that held the clothing. It was a gruesome representation of a human being.

She changed all the lights with bulbs that flashed and flickered. She laughed softly as she continued the chore at hand with pleasure. When she was beside the bed, she pulled the covers down. She took out the jar of spiders and poured them on her sheets and then pulled the covers back up. As Cheryl walked over to the dresser, she saw a picture of Marcus and Amanda together. She cringed, pulling the picture off the mirror. Marcus was behind Amanda, staring at the camera and embracing her. Cheryl couldn't contain herself. She flicked Amanda's face with her index finger. "Enjoy while you can. He won't be yours for long." Cheryl was about to put the picture back, but then thought better of it. She tore the photo in half, splitting Marcus and Amanda apart from each other. She rolled up the top end that contained Marcus's face and placed it in her front pocket, tapping the picture lightly as she continued with her chore with delight. She turned the lights off in the room and pressed the button on her flashlight so she could see.

She attached a string between the window and the rocking chair to make it appear like it was moving when she attempted to close the window. She even took one of Amanda's red lipsticks and drew a small line between the chin and neck of Amanda's torn picture. She then placed it back on the mirror. She had an old box that screamed when anyone walked past the sensors strategically positioned under the bed. Cheryl rolled up her sleeves for the next step. She took a jar of fake blood and squeezed the tube on some of Amanda's clothes in the closet. She looked down in her bag yet again, looking for other treasures. She was so engrossed into her task that she didn't hear anyone come into the house. She heard the floor boards creak in the hallway. She stopped what she was doing and then crawled into the closet and shut the door. "Damn it."

She turned off the flashlight and tried to stay quiet. She could hear the footsteps getting louder. It sounded as though the person stopped right by the bedroom door. She listened to the sound of children snickering, and then it changed into a woman's evil cackle. The noise echoed throughout the room into the closet that she hid in. She knew no one had seen her, so she continued to be quiet, waiting for what would happen next. She thought she heard the sound of something dragging across the floor.

"Damn," she cursed softly. Cheryl forgot that she left the bag on the floor by the bed. The strangest thing was that the sensor didn't go off. She didn't hear the scream that usually blared from the box. Did she turn the blasted thing on? She couldn't remember. She could feel the vibration of a thud on the floor. Cheryl's heart increased its beating. *What the heck was that?* she thought. She wanted to look through the keyhole but was afraid to, not knowing what was on the other side. The only sound that came after that was a door shutting loudly. Cheryl took a deep breath of relief and waited a few more minutes. She placed her hand on the doorknob when she was certain that no one was there. She opened the door just a crack to take a good look around. It seemed as though the unknown person was gone. She looked down on the floor where she left her bag. It was gone. She racked her brain quickly, trying to remember if she left anything in there that could incriminate her. She thought quickly of what to do before the person returned. She saw the opened window. Cheryl could hear someone coming back. It sounded like loud chattering and clawing. The noise was like someone was crawling fast on hands and knees.

Cheryl was certain that whoever it was knew that someone was in the house. As she listened to the scratching on the door, she covered her ears. She stood still when she heard the growl as the door moved, violently, from someone's hard rapping on the opposite side. She turned her gaze away from the door slightly, looking at the window and balcony for escape. As she began to move toward the opening, she fell on the floor hard from the canola oil she had poured on the ground earlier. She cradled her arm, rubbing it a bit from the fall. Before she could think about it thoroughly, she went for it. She ran to the window and began climbing down the trellis that was attached to the house. It was all in good timing, because Cheryl heard the door open with a loud slam against the wall that cradled the door frame. She could still hear the sound of a woman's evil laughter as she continued to climb downward. She continued quickly before the person realized that she was scaling the outside wall. The thorns on the roses bit into her fingers, making them bleed. She was so afraid that she didn't feel the sting until she felt the grass beneath her feet. She peered at her hands to get a good look at the damage.

Cheryl's heart began to settle and the adrenaline that coursed through her veins subsided. With a little laugh she looked up at the window to see an eerie silhouette, but nothing was said. Cheryl shook her fist. "You didn't get me." She laughed again in triumph. She turned her eyes away from the person and straightened her clothes. She couldn't understand why the person was still on the balcony in the darkness. Why didn't he or she give chase? She then felt the tug on her ankles. Cheryl was pulled face down to the ground. Digging her fingernails into grass was no safe haven for her. With a loud scream, Cheryl was quickly pulled through the open window to the basement. As she cried out one last time for help, the window closed, leaving her plea unheard.

Chapter 19

When we move into the future we come across facts and events that change our lives forever, sometimes for better, and sometimes for worse. I have seen better. You never think that it could happen to you. The young always have that attitude of immortality. It is that small lining that makes us impulsive and daring. When something like this happens, reality sets in, giving us that sense of caution and fear. That time came for me today. We always question why me or why now? I try to stay focused and believe that everything in life has a reason. What was mine? I racked my brain, still thinking that all this was just some terrifying dream and soon I would wake up. After the revelation of my family's past secrets, I decided to take a cab. As I looked out the window into the sky, I continuously asked those very questions to whoever was listening up there. I know they will always remain unanswered, but one can't fault me for trying. I cursed myself for a life of naivety. How, after all this time, had I not noticed the signs? In the back of mind, did I always know and decided to ignore it? Is unawareness bliss? I am not so sure it is. The truth hit home, and it struck me hard today. I was still trying to adjust to the cruel reality of it.

The moon was full and surrounded by a red luminous light. It seemed to call out a warning of caution and foreboding. I took the fetish from my pocket and stared at it curiously. I held it by its string with my thumb and index finger, waiting for it to show its hidden stories. It was as elusive as the night itself. The darkness beyond the window symbolized my thoughts and feelings. When would the light come back? I missed my dad. This was the time that I needed him the most. I covered my face in grief and self-pity. I was lost, and there wasn't anyone who could help me or even begin to understand. Maybe I went too far today. Maybe I shouldn't have bombarded Ivy with all those questions. The truth needed to be told. Didn't it? I didn't ask for this. I didn't want whatever this was. I looked out the window to the outside world again.

"Dad, where are you?" I asked again in a choked sob. I held onto the only thing I had left of him, his coat. The dark, black leather jacket embraced me back as I hugged myself.

I resented Toby for not telling me about this long ago, but then again, if he did tell me, would I have believed him? Probably not. I guess this was my purpose. I laughed sarcastically, still thinking that I should be committed. I didn't know where to go. Toby was not with me. He knew I was angry. He left me to give me time to absorb and cope. I was alone, a prisoner of my thoughts. I wouldn't let the tears fall. I tried to maintain control of my feelings.

It wasn't time to cry; it was time to come up with a plan. I regretted leaving Mom at the house as I did. I was certain that she was worried. I looked at my watch with an intake of breath. It was getting late, and I didn't want Mom to be by herself tonight. I looked at my phone to see that the service had been turned off. I knew then that I was in deep trouble, not by unknown forces or natural disasters, but by none other than Mom.

Whatever was going on in that house, it was abundantly clear that it was getting stronger. Was Nanny Ivy right? Was the house's internal source coming for me? Was it me who breathed life back into the structure by my abilities? People had been dying and going missing in that house for years. I remembered something that Daphne had said.

As the cab continued to move, the driver asked, "Where to, kid?"

"High Street Public Library."

The cabbie looked in his rearview mirror with a look of shock. "I don't know if it's open now, girly."

"I need to get there."

The driver shrugged with indifference. "It's your money." He was tired of the silence and started up a conversation. "You're new around these parts, aren't you?"

I hesitated before answering, "How did you guess?"

The elderly man laughed. "Thought so. There are a little over six thousand that live around this area. There are thirty-three people per square mile. Only the locals come to town. Not very many tourists, I am afraid." He nodded in the mirror. "Where did you move to?"

"Water Street," I responded with a sigh.

He looked closer in the rearview mirror. "You're not that family that moved into the old Warwick house, are you?"

I nodded.

The man gave a little chuckle. "Your family is pretty brave. A lot of the old timers won't set foot on that property, not to mention the teenagers."

"So I hear."

"So is it true what they say?" he asked out of curiosity.

Amanda pretended that she didn't hear the question.

The cabbie took a long breath. "It's as I thought. You'll probably move out soon. No one ever stays there long."

"I don't know about that," I responded daringly. "You never know; the place might grow on us."

The driver laughed. "Somehow I highly doubt that."

He stopped in front of the building. "Do you want me to wait till you get in, just in case its closed?"

"Yes, thanks."

I was happy to see that my traveling wasn't for nothing. The door opened when I pulled the handle forward. I waved to the cab driver and watched him as he drove off.

I smiled sweetly as I walked to the front desk and asked where the old newspapers were. I was directed downstairs to a machine to view old newspaper articles. I sat in silence as I listened to the old machine hum its tune, letting me know that it was still in working order. I stopped when I saw the article about the Warwick's dated back from 1960. The headlines read Mysterious Death at 210 Water Street. I decided to read more.

Mrs. Ilene Warwick was found dead yesterday in the basement of her family home after an anonymous call to the Ellsworth Police Department. It is unclear at this time if the caller had any involvement in the killing. According to the coroner's office, Mrs. Warwick was murdered around 3:00 Saturday morning. She was allegedly stabbed 50 times and placed in a small crawl space beneath the residence. Mr. Warwick gave no comment when questioned. In a statement to the district police department, Mr. Warwick claimed he was in Rome at the time of the murder. It is also unclear of the whereabouts of Drake Warwick, age 13, who has been missing since the slaying.

Detective Felding of the Ellsworth Police Department stated that there are no suspects at this time. One source stated the house was locked up and there were no indications of forced entry. The most baffling part of this case was the fact that all the windows of the home were reportedly boarded up from the inside. The search still continues for the child who may be the only answer to this mystery of who killed Mrs. Warwick and why.

As I continued the go through the articles, I stopped at a photo. I sat a moment in silence as I gazed at the picture. It was a photograph of Drake Warwick. "No, it couldn't be." The picture looked like the person that was in the house the night I was attacked. "It can't be." The photo staring back at me was Drake, asking me for help. The distorted figure was a thirteen-year-old boy. I saw the name Felding again. I thought about the police officer that came to the hospital to question me about my attack. Was he related to this detective? It had been thirty-one years since a family lived in that house. I inhaled in shock as I read more articles of the property's past. As I moved further back in the town history, I became appalled that the house still stood. There were lists of murders, suicides, death by natural causes, and disappearances. There was even a story about a group of teens that went missing around the seven acres that I lived on. All that was found was their abandoned car on the street. When I tried to go further, when the town was called Sumner, the screen went blank. I frowned in confusion and then I went to the front desk in a shaken state to ask about the information.

"I am sorry, hon," the librarian stated. "That's as far back as our records can go."

"I don't understand," I questioned.

"There was a town fire back then. Most of the documents at the hall of records and the library were destroyed. That is as far back as we can go; sorry."

"How about the census records? Were they burned as well?"

"Yes, hon, that was one of the reasons why we changed the name. I guess the town folk figured they would try to start anew."

"Or hide something," I mumbled under my breath.

I thanked her for her time and left the building. When I stood outside, I didn't know what to do. I looked at my watch again. I pounded my forehead with the heel of my hand. Marcus was going to meet me at the house this evening.

Lauren sat in front of Officer Felding and Trent Shikoba. Trent thought it was best that Ellsworth's finest explain about the house where she resided. Trent drove Lauren to the police department so she could hear it from him personally. She sat in silence as Derek told some of the history of the house. She couldn't believe her ears.

"I thought it was just one incident with one family."

"No, Ms. Pennington. There were others," Felding stated, correcting her.

"Does Julie Warwick know about all this?" Lauren asked.

"It was Julie's uncle that originally owned the house. Tim Warwick killed himself after the death of his wife and his son's disappearance." Officer Felding shrugged. "Julie inherited the house after her grandfather died. She was the only heir to the property. Her grandfather kept the story quiet. He was worried about the scandal on the family name, because Tim was a prime suspect in the murder. Her grandfather would have kept that from her. No one has been in the house since. He closed it up and let it fall apart, hoping the city would condemn it. He wanted to demolish that house, but couldn't."

"Why?" Lauren asked, confused.

"That house is a historical place. When a home is listed as such, you cannot change anything about the property unless the town allows it. His permit was denied," Derek said.

"They allowed me to work on it."

Derek responded, "That is because you're restoring the home to its original state. That is different. When you try to change the layout, that's when the historical society becomes difficult about the request. Mr. Warwick wanted to destroy it."

"Ms. Pennington, your home was the very first building that started the town," Trent added. "People fear the land, but they won't destroy it. It's part of the town's beginnings. Your house was also one of the only six houses that survived the great flood in 1923. It made the committee want to keep it all the more."

"It's just a house, Trent." Officer Felding was becoming agitated as time went on, and Trent knew it. "If you two don't mind, I have real cases to take care of and important work to do." Derek opened his office door. "I am sorry to waste your time, Ms. Pennington. I can't do anything until Amanda has been missing for twenty-four hours. All I can suggest is for you to go home at this time. If she still hasn't come home by morning, call us."

Lauren just nodded.

Trent gazed at Officer Felding and spoke in a condescending tone. "If I didn't know any better, it sounded to me like the officer isn't at all sympathetic to the situation at hand." Trent stood up. "I hope for your sake that she does come home. You can at least keep an eye out." It looked as though Trent was getting his point across.

Derek didn't want to cross paths with Shikoba. Those that did always ended up compromised. "I'll tell you what," Derek said before they walked out the room. "I'll let the guys in the department know about Amanda. If we see her, we'll pick her up. That's all I can do for now."

"Thank you, Officer Felding," Lauren began. "I didn't want to cause any trouble."

Derek looked at Shikoba when he made his statement with a smile, not taking his eyes off of him. "No trouble, Ms. Pennington. We are happy to serve the public."

With that last remark, Lauren walked out with Trent following her lead.

"Geez," he whispered out of frustration. Derek rubbed his face, praying for strength.

Derek went over to his file cabinet. He stared at the top drawer. He turned and looked out the window to his right, watching Lauren and Trent leave the station. He looked again to the drawer and pulled out a file. Derek held the file in his hands, feeling its weight. The distant past recorded on its pages brought great heaviness on his conscience. He closed the drawer smartly, listening to the echo of it closing. He crossed over to his desk and stood silently. He contemplated before sitting down. With a heavy heart he dropped the file down on his table and then opened it slowly. It was the last case his father worked, long ago. Derek's father was so obsessed with it he kept it close at hand. It was one of a few cases that Derek's father couldn't forget about, let alone solve. He looked through the brittle notes with care as his father did and read intensely, hoping to find something that was missed.

Officer Felding continued looking at crime scene photos and eyewitness testimonies. Nothing matched or made sense. The commotion outside his door was breaking his concentration. He stood up quickly and slammed the door closed. It was not as loud as he hoped it would be, but it was enough. Derek marched over to his chair and quietly looked over the file. Each flip of the page brought back the memories of a boy whose father was always engrossed in work. Derek could now understand the compulsion that confined his father to this office. His light blond curls circled around his fingers as he stroked the curls back behind his ears in frustration. "Ilene Warwick and her missing son, Drake," he said as he went into his drawer and pulled out a bottle. He took out a plastic cup and poured himself a drink. He drank it down quickly and then looked at the last photo. He gazed at Tim Warwick's death scene two weeks later. "Poor sod." Mr. Warwick had hanged himself in the family room by the fireplace.

Derek raised it into the light so he could get a better look at the picture. "Were you grieving?" he asked the picture, waiting for a response. "Or couldn't you accept the fact that you murdered her?" There was no doubt in his mind that Mr. Warwick did it. It wasn't a secret that Ilene had affairs in the town. Derek's father was included in that long list of men in her life. When the news hit the papers, so did the rumors of Ilene's secrets. Derek scoffed out loud as he remembered the day his mother left when she was told about her husband's affair. Derek was all his father had left. His father kept Derek, and his mother couldn't get custody. What chance did she have against the local town sheriff? Derek hated him for that. The days after that grew worse, leaving Derek alone at home as his father worked late and dwelt on old cases. He stared at the cause of his miserable childhood. It seemed like an open-and-shut case, didn't it? Derek's father didn't think so. For Derek's father, Joseph, it was something Mr. Warwick said during interrogation.

Derek pulled out an old tape that wobbled in the file, weighing it as he held it up to the light, deliberating if he should play it once again. He pulled out the tape recorder and listened once more, entranced in its mysteries like his father once was. He sat in quiet contemplation, waiting to hear something that he missed.

"Don't you think I knew about the men? It was a mutual arrangement between Ilene and me. We just stayed together and had our equal share of sport. Ilene never loved me. She loved my money. I wouldn't have ever hurt her. I am not a killer. I am being framed. Can't you see that? It's that house. Ilene hated that house." Derek rubbed his face as he listened to the old tape. He heard Tim sob. "My son. You have to find my son." Derek heard the slam of the man's hand against the table, letting out his frustrations and fear for his child. "He's still in that house. You hear me? You've got to find him. You have to before...before it does."

Derek was silent as he listened closely, hanging on every word spoken. It was Joseph who spoke next, "Before who does?"

"You wouldn't believe me if I told you."

"Mr. Warwick, I know that you come from an important family. Is there someone you know that would do this? Do you know who has your son?"

There was a brief pause on the tape, and then Warwick said, "Ahote."

"Do you know where this person is?"

Tim became more agitated with the questioning. Derek could tell as the old tape continued. "I don't know where he is or who he is," he screamed out. "His name was written on the walls in my house. You've seen it as well. It was written in blood. I heard one of your deputies say the tests came back, and it wasn't Ilene's blood. I should have never moved my family into that house," he said in self-pity. "I should have listened to the old man."

"Listened to who, Mr. Warwick?"

"I don't know," he screamed out. "Some old man came to the house when we moved in."

"What did this old man say?"

"He said we shouldn't be there. He said the land was not meant to be lived on, or something like that. He talked about bad spirits. Stuff like that. I thought he was a crazy old loon, so I shooed him off the property. Oh, God forgive me. Even when the weird stuff happened, I refused to see it. Ilene was always at home with Drake. She would call when I was away, talking crazy things about ghosts and the supernatural. I thought she was becoming ill. At one time I was ready to have her committed. I think that's why she was with other men, so she wasn't alone. It's all my fault. I should have taken them from that house when Ilene wanted to leave. I told her this was her home and to get a hold of herself. Even Drake was scared. Have you seen the medical reports about his injuries? They thought that Ilene was hitting the kid, but he said continuously it wasn't her."

"Who was hitting your son, Mr. Warwick? Was it you?"

"No, it wasn't me. The kid wouldn't tell me, he was

too scared."

"So you left your family in a house even though they didn't feel safe, Mr. Warwick?"

"Yes, I did. Sounds like crazy talk when your wife says your house is haunted."

"You should have gotten her help."

"Well, detective, she didn't crawl into a small crawl space herself and break all her bones doing so, did she?"

Derek couldn't hear any sincerity in Warwick's voice, just hatred. "Please officer, just find my boy. I know he's in that house. I just know it."

Derek pressed the stop button and didn't continue any further. Tim Warwick did eventually get out. His father paid a hefty bail bond, and Tim stayed in that house, convinced that his son was still there. Why? Did he know something more than what he stated to the police? Who was Ahote? Derek had a feeling that the old man that Tim talked about was probably Trent's father. He could feel it in his bones. Derek continued to flip through the old pages looking for any statements or affidavits about the mysterious old man. There was nothing further on it. Derek couldn't find any reports.

He sat up straighter in his chair and rubbed his chin with his index finger. "Maybe it is about time I paid Grandfather Shikoba a visit." With that last remark, Derek slammed the file shut, unsatisfied with all its contents.

Chapter 20

Marcus arrived at Amanda's house just like he promised but was surprised to see all the lights out. He turned off his motorcycle and removed his helmet, pulling his hair back to see better. It was quiet. A little too quiet. He couldn't even hear any calls of Mother Nature's creatures in the dark night. If the old man taught Marcus one thing it was that when even nature discontinues her cries in the darkness, something was off balance. Marcus made his eyes into slits as he tried to assess the situation. It was getting too dark, and it didn't seem like anyone was home. The silence was putting him on edge. As he looked at the front door, he saw that it was slightly ajar. He thought for a moment that he heard Amanda in the house, calling him. He removed himself from his seat, and leaned his bike on its kickstand, and stood, waiting for the voice again.

Going against his gut feeling, he spoke out to her. "Amanda, is that you?" He waited.

Marcus heard it again, but it was too faint to tell who it was. It sounded feminine. Marcus thought he heard someone say "Help."

A twinge of panic began to course through his veins, yet he still held his ground, waiting for the unknown voice to speak again. As he looked around, it seemed as though the leaves had fallen off all the trees, leaving them as bare and ominous as the house they surrounded. He looked down and closed his eyes briefly, listening and waiting. He knew better than to react too quickly. He had to admit that his grandfather's stories might seem a bit farfetched, but if Aki said the stories were true, then Marcus believed him. He had never done anything to make Marcus not have faith him. Living with his grandfather, Marcus had seen enough paranormal things that he couldn't explain.

As he continued to listen in the distance, it brought him back to the memory of a child that was possessed by a demon spirit. The entity was driving the child mad. Aki removed the entity and sent it back to the spirit world. Was the child mentally ill? Marcus didn't know, but what he did know was that the child was healthy and cured after the entity was removed, with no relapses.

Marcus brought his thoughts back to his present state. His intuition told him to stay where he was. He still waited.

He jumped when he felt something slowly entangling his legs. As he looked down, to his relief it was a cat. He grinned as he bent down to pick the bundle up in his arms. He stroked the feline's dirty tan and black coat as it purred loudly in satisfaction.

"Are you Taboo?" The cat meowed loudly in response. "Amanda has been looking for you. Where have you been?" He continued to stroke the dirty ball of fur. They both seemed happy to find each other. Taboo continued with his happy tune, digging his nails into Marcus's arms, but that feeling was short lived. Taboo's ears erected, and the purring discontinued. Marcus felt the change in the atmosphere as well. They both turned their sights on the house. A slight smell of decay surrounded them. Taboo began to hiss with dissatisfaction. As the cat growled, Marcus tried to put him at ease.

"It's okay." The animal didn't seem settled.

That's when he heard the scream that emanated from the depths of a hollow prison. He felt the blood drain from his face. The chill moved from the back of his neck and down his spine. It was not only a cry of fear but of pain as well. Marcus didn't think; he acted quickly. "Amanda," Marcus shouted as he dropped the cat and ran through the front entrance. He started to climb the stairs. He turned when he heard the front door slam hard, cracking the wooden door frame. The house began to creak and groan as if awakened from a long slumber. The floor vibrated, shaking the wooden boards. Marcus couldn't maintain his stance. He lost his footing and started to tumble. Marcus groaned with each step he hit. He reached out, trying to grip anything to stop the fall downward. It was happening so fast he couldn't stop it. When he hit the bottom, he sat up, trying to regain his faculties.

Marcus held his forehead and then jumped with an intake of breath. When he released his forehead he looked down at the palm of his right hand to see the evidence of injury. He stared at the blood in a dazed state and then tried to stand. He wasn't ready, he quickly realized, as he fell back into a sitting position on the first step. He gazed around, looking for some sign of where Amanda could be. He thought he heard a slight whisper. "Amanda?" The front door opened, giving Marcus the chance for a quick escape, but he didn't take it. He went in the opposite direction down the hall, where he heard the voice. Marcus's ears rang from the fall. He cleared his throat as he shouted again for the Pennington girl. He turned and peered down the basement stairs, looking for the source of the voice. He felt for the light switch and then turned on the light. The light glowed brightly and then flickered like a candle in the wind, but it didn't extinguish. Marcus stumbled down the first few steps and then continued to the room below.

The light above him hung freely from a wire, swinging side to side like a pendulum. His attention on the light distracted him, for certain corners of the room remained dark. To see better, he raised his hand to still the swinging bulb. When the light was still, he looked out. The old musty basement filled his nose with a pungent odor of mildew and age. The floor beneath him was bare earth. The uneven soil made Marcus stagger toward the sandstone foundation. As his hands touched the old structure, the mortar in between its joints crumbled under Marcus's fingertips. Dusty powder filled the space surrounding him, making him inhale the substance and cough loudly.

The smell in the room transformed into an aroma of urine. The foul stench made him gag slightly as he covered his mouth. His gaze darted upward when he heard a whisper again. It sounded like a group of people talking. He jumped when he saw a chair in corner of the room with someone sitting in it. He could hear the sound of scratching, like nails digging into the chair. He thought he saw the head that bowed to him convulse quickly, but he attributed it to the trick of the light.

Marcus took a step closer. The head of the person rose quickly and stared at him with a sinister sneer. "Cheryl?" he asked in confusion. Marcus moved closer in concern, but Cheryl still remained seated, unmoving. She was covered in dirt and soot. Her eyes were black and blue. She moved her head from side to side. He could hear the popping sound of her neck joints snap back into place. It seemed as though her eye color had changed.

When she spoke, it sounded like more than one person. "Hello, Marcus." The dark eyes looked out further and smiled. "Nadie Shikoba."

Grandfather Shikoba woke up in a sweat. His heart continued to pound in his chest. He rubbed his hands. He stood up quickly and picked up his cell phone. He cursed loudly in his language as he tried to remember how to work the thing. Grandfather Shikoba never used the cell phone. Marcus made him take it for emergencies. If there ever was one, this would be it. He reached out for the scrap piece of paper that had the directions of the phone's functions. His hopes disappeared when Marcus failed to answer. He then tried Trent. "Is Marcus with you?"

I took another cab and decided to go back to the house. I knew what was waiting for me. I didn't know what was worse, an angry spirit or an angry mother. Toby finally decided to join me. "Are you still angry with me?"

I crossed my arms and stared at the taxi driver. I looked at Toby. "All the years I think back to what people probably thought of me, talking to thin air."

He laughed out loud, "It wasn't all that bad. Amanda, people talk to themselves every day. Not even Mom suspected."

"You should have told me a long time ago." I raised my hand and touched his face. "Why are you so real to me?"

He shrugged. "We always seem real to the Obeahs."

I hit him hard. "What is that supposed to mean?"

He smiled. "Interested? Does that mean we are back on speaking terms?"

I shrugged.

"The Obeahs were a society of Egyptians. They were called witches and sorcerers, but they were more than that. They believed in magic, and they could do things no other people could."

"See dead people," I finished.

"I hear that our origins are from the race of Atlantis. I was told there are not many of us left. Only one is born for every generation. Some say that the Obeahs can even talk to God."

I sighed. "Who did you hear that from?"

"Nan. She told me a lot of things. Like, did you know why you have Taboo?"

"Because I love her, and she was a stray."

Toby shook his head negatively. "Taboo found you. You didn't find her. She chose you, to protect you from the unseen." He enunciated every word for effect. "The Egyptians called them *Ubasti*. Some thought them evil, but in reality they harbor a good that forces spirits away. Your Siamese is your guardian."

I held my head in my hands. "First crazy kid and then ghost buster, and now I am a witch."

"You're not a witch. You're an Obeah. There's a difference. There is no true English translation for what you are. It is the only thing that comes close. Witches and sorcerers came much later, but our group started the practices."

I stared at him with skepticism. "It all seems like a made-up story."

"You feel that way 'cause Mom raised you to be a

realist. She lived around all the superstitions and stories most of her life. Mom believes in only what she sees. She can't see me, Amanda. Mom will not accept it until she experiences it herself. She will never understand. She couldn't even understand Dad."

I held the fetish in my hand and then squeezed it tightly.

Toby grabbed my shoulder as I told the cab to stop in front of the old gates to the house. "Nan doesn't want you to go back there. She said it isn't safe."

As I opened the door, I looked up at Toby. "Mom's there; I have to go."

"That will be twenty-five dollars please," the cabbie said, getting my attention before I closed the door. I gave the cabbie his money, not realizing I left my father's jacket on the back seat of his car.

Toby still stayed where he was. He left with the taxi driver. As Toby watched Amanda cross the barrier toward the house, Toby fled quickly to get Ivy.

Chapter 21

I approached the front of the house and noticed Marcus's motorcycle. Mom's car was gone, and all the lights in the house were off. The leaves had spilled on the ground, concealing the land beneath it. I inhaled the fragrance of the cold air, praying for inner peace of mind. The bare trees seemed to come alive of their own accord. They spoke their own language as their branches screeched against the house and window panes. I thought of the poor boy that had gone missing in the house years ago. Will that be my fate? The front door was open, welcoming me to my fate. I didn't see Marcus, but I could feel something was wrong. I looked down as my feet hit the front porch when I heard the sound of a cat. "Taboo." I placed the fetish in my pocket, and then I grabbed the fur ball in my arms and held her tight.

I scolded her, holding her out in front of me as she purred. "Where have you been?" I placed her cold nose to mine and stared deeply into her eyes. "Don't ever scare me like that again." I hugged her again, this time a bit too tight. She let me know, with a loud meow. I was happy she was okay. I hadn't seen her in weeks. "What have you been eating? Rodents?" I smelled her and held my nose. "You need a bath, buddy." The cat responded with a low sound of disapproval, knowing full well I would attempt it. They say cats clean themselves, but this cat needed a bit of help.

I closed the door behind me and went to turn on the light, but it wouldn't turn on. I then felt it like Taboo did. It was an energy that prickled the lower back and tingled all of my senses. I felt a headache overtaking me, making my head pound. Taboo placed her paws on my shoulder, trying to give me some support. She could feel it too. I knew she could. The cat jumped from my chest and scurried toward the basement stairs. I could tell she wanted to go there. "What is it, Taboo?"

The cat scratched the door like a dog, trying to make her statement known. I opened the door and moved down, following her. With my last step, I looked in the direction of the cat. I ran over when I saw Marcus standing still, staring at something. "Marcus, what are you——" I didn't get to finish my question as I moved beside him and looked out. Cheryl stood there looking like a rag doll.

Marcus held my hand steadfast. "Don't move. It's not Cheryl."

"What? Of course it's Cheryl. What's going on?"

My cat moved in front of us. Cheryl's face changed, and she screamed. Marcus pushed me behind him as we slowly moved back to the foot of the stairs. I couldn't see what was happening. Marcus was a lot stronger than I was. He continued to force my body back. I heard Taboo hiss.

I couldn't help looking over Marcus's shoulder. I couldn't believe what I was witnessing. Cheryl jumped back, leapt up, and clutched the ceiling, screeching and hissing. Marcus held my arms tighter and ushered me up the stairs slowly. We bolted into a run at the top. When we hit the hallway, the door shut along with all the other doors in the house. Marcus pulled out his cell phone as we started to walk quickly from room to room to find a way out.

Marcus shouted in frustration. "Amanda, my phone isn't working. Try yours."

I grabbed my phone out of my pocket, frantically fumbling to call. Mine was the same. I couldn't get a signal. "Where are the phones in the house?"

"The closest is in the dining room, across the hall," I pointed in the direction for effect. He took my hand and pulled me toward the room. The house was so big, it felt like it was swallowing us whole. The house was creaking and moaning in displeasure as we tried to find a means of escape.

Marcus picked up the receiver to find no dial tone. "It's dead." He slammed the phone back into its cradle and looked around. I thought I heard Cheryl scream below. Marcus looked as horrified as I was. We tried the windows. They wouldn't open. Marcus took one of the dining room chairs and attempted to break a window. He didn't get close enough to the glass. The chair was pulled out from his grasp and flew in the opposite direction, hitting the wall behind us.

I turned, seeing a shadow at the corner of my eye. I embraced Marcus in fright. "Did you see that?"

I could tell Marcus was as scared as I was, but he rubbed my arms for comfort. We scooted down in the darkness with our backs pressed against the wall. "Our best bet is to try to stay quiet," he whispered. "I'll get us out of here."

I nodded slowly. I looked back in the direction where I had seen the shadow. I was paralyzed as I saw it in front of my face, staring back at me. There was no body, just eyes. I tried not to breathe, but it knew I could see it. Marcus pulled me tighter to him.

"We have to go now," I said in a wavering voice. "It knows where we are." Marcus couldn't see it.

Just when I thought the eyes could not get any closer, they did. They looked deeper into me, as if trying to read me. It felt as though it was draining the life from my body when it made contact. The room seemed cool and empty. All I could think about was finding a way to escape. I couldn't scream or talk. It began to growl like an animal. Marcus pulled me up, hearing the noise. He could feel the icy air as well. He guided me toward the stairs quickly, trying to escape from what he couldn't see. We ran up the stairs to the first door we came to. It was Toby's room. The door gave way, opening to my persistence. When we were inside, Marcus shut the door softly, trying not to attract attention. He moved to the window instantly. He tried to push the window upward. It was as if the windowpane was nailed shut, as if an unknown force forbade its opening. I handed him the fetish as I looked around. "What are you doing?" he asked breathlessly.

"I am looking for something to wedge the door. Help me."

Marcus helped search for something to barricade the door. He started by pushing the large dresser across the wall to the door. When it was properly placed, he pushed it forward toward the door frame, fitting it tightly to where the frame touched the back of the dresser.

Marcus looked out the window to see a large tree in close proximity to the house. He sized up the large branch that reached out toward the window, whispering its promise for escape. I stepped away from the door when I heard the sound of the door handle turning. The door didn't open right away, because it was locked. When I heard the click and the sound of the door hitting the dresser forcefully, I ran to Marcus's side.

Marcus decided to use his own method. He rammed his elbow through the glass, breaking it. When the glass opening wouldn't give way, he kicked it soundly with his boot. The opening shattered and then flew open with such force that the remnants of the frame hit the outside ground below them.

The lightning from the storm outside flickered, lighting the room briefly, and then we were back in the darkness. The rain came in a downpour. He moved closer to me and held out his hand to me. I couldn't help staring. Even now his actions showed what I meant to him. He helped me over the side. I couldn't help looking at him and his deep blue eyes. I watched the rain drop fall onto his face down his chin. The urgency in his stare did not need words. He rubbed my arms quickly and hugged me slightly for encouragement. Even in the dim night I could still see him. I shivered as his eyes peered into mine. I could feel a stirring within my soul. My heart continued to skip a beat as he looked at me. Even with everything that was happening around us, we continued staring at each other. My hand shook as I touched his face. He steadied it as he enclosed my hand with his own. The warmth of his hand calmed me and made me steady.

Marcus was here. Even now, through all this mess, he was here. He leaned his forehead onto mine. He didn't break eye contact, not for one second. It was at that moment that I came to a realization. It was that single instant that led me to an epiphany. I felt it within. It was a forbidden truth of my subconscious mind.

I was in love. I was completely and deeply in love with Marcus Shikoba. We broke apart when we heard a crash. With all seriousness, he said, "I will be there. Don't look back and keep moving." He took his jacket off and wrapped it tightly around me, holding my face in his hands. I placed one arm inside the sleeve and gripped tightly to the wooden sill that held my weight. His face was back, so close to mine. I could feel his breath on my lips, warming them.

I nodded my head and kissed him. He held my weight as I stepped out toward the large branch. I stumbled a bit when I stepped onto the old dogwood limb. I slipped, falling on top of the branch. My chest hit the tree limb soundly, taking my breath away. I hugged the tree tightly, so I wouldn't fall off. I closed my eyes and took in the pain that followed when chest connected to the branch beneath me. I heard Marcus's intake of breath, so I turned briefly to reassure him that I was all right. I regained my balance and I began to crawl across to the center of the tree. I hugged it as though it was a long lost friend. I felt the bark scrape my cheek, but I didn't care. I was happy to have made it across. I smiled, looking back to see how close Marcus was. He wasn't there. "Marcus," I cried out. The storm drowned out my cry. I couldn't hear him or see him. The rain blinded me. I placed my hand in Marcus's, pocket hoping to find his phone. All that was there was the fetish. I pulled it from his jacket. "Toby, help me." I waited but he didn't come. I looked up into the heavens, praying for an answer. None came. When Toby didn't appear. I did what I thought was right. I did what I felt I had to do. I placed the bear back into Marcus's jacket, and I went back.

SHADOWS

Ivy was terrified. She was never so scared in her life. She held her necklace that held a large crucifix. Whenever she was rattled, it was one thing she did. It was calming to her. With thumb and index finger, she picked the cross up, holding the chain against her lips as she moved the object back and forth. She looked over to her bag beside her. She could only hope she had everything. She couldn't shake the feeling of death. She shivered from the thought. Yes, there was a death. She knew it. Toby was ahead of Ivy. He could get back to the house faster than she could. As she looked down, she couldn't believe what she saw. "Excuse me, sir, have you dropped anyone off on Water Street today?"

"Sure did. It was about an hour or so ago. There are only three of us working tonight. Ellsworth is a small town. Why do you ask?'

"No reason." Ivy clasped onto the jacket that once belonged to her son. She was choked up with emotion when she touched it. She recognized it well. She bought it for him. It was the last thing he ever received from Ivy. Her eyes clouded with tears as she held the cold leather with her fingertips. "I hope it's not too late."

"Stop your fretting, Ivy."

"Mam, not now."

"You know you are ill-prepared for this one. You couldn't save Lucas. You need to stop this. He made his decision. "

"Mam always knows best."

"Smudging sticks and chanting isn't going to make this go away, Ivy."

"Then what do you suggest, mam?"

Mother smiled sweetly. "You can first stop your bloody blabbering and soften your loud tone. The cabbie is looking at you."

Ivy smiled at the cab driver as he quickly looked down and returned his eyes to the road.

"You are out of you element, Ivy. Just get Amanda out of that house. You cannot clear the negative energies that reside there. It is a lost cause. That land will eat you alive. Once inside, I cannot help you."

"I don't want to argue anymore. Go help your grandson while I think."

When Ivy realized that her mother was gone, she noticed the driver was staring again. "Mothers; they are completely impossible." The more he stared, the more agitated Ivy became. She stared out the window briefly and then looked back to the cabbie. "You know, your father wants me to tell you to get a real job, and stand up to that wife of yours. He said, 'Noah, you were always a mama's boy.'"

The cab driver was confused. "I am sorry, miss, did you know my father?"

Ivy didn't respond.

"My father has been dead for a few years now."

"Exactly."

The cabbie didn't want to know. He just wanted to get the crazy woman out of his car as quickly as he could. He increased his speed to shorten his time with her. Ivy put the coat neatly in her lap.

"Lucas, your baby needs you."

Chapter 22

Toby was where he wished to be. He stood in front of the old Victorian. He knew Amanda was near; he could feel it. He could also feel other things. They were like voices that called out to him, begging him to come closer. If he closed his eyes, he could feel the inner pull, their wanting of his essence. The sounds seemed beautiful, beckoning like the siren to a lost sailor with her songs of pleasures. As he moved to the door, he could smell the stench of blood and decay. He noticed Marcus's bike parked out front. The quiet was nerve-racking, stirring his emotions with fear and loss. He remained as he was, waiting for Amanda's call.

"Amanda, where are you?" he shouted.

Toby knew that Amanda had control of what she could see. She just didn't realize it. Maybe she was right. He shouldn't have kept this secret from her this long. Maybe it was for selfish reasons. He didn't want to die. He wanted more than anything to be alive. To feel, taste, touch, and breathe. He couldn't understand why a lot of the living prayed for death. Death was isolation and loneliness, especially if you were stuck between this world and heaven. Toby scoffed, feeling sorry for himself. He felt cheated, never fully knowing what it was like to be full of life. He envied Amanda greatly for her life. He would never know what it was like to feel the wind across his face, a real kiss, or true emotions. At times it seemed trivial, but it looked so beneficial. He would never know what pain felt like. He couldn't ever embrace his mother that he missed and loved so dearly or hear her say "I love you." He would grieve if he could, but he didn't know how. If only he were alive long enough to experience it.

Toby turned from the front door as he thought more about his mother. The only thought his mother ever had for him was sorrow. He remembered one time wandering into her room when his father was still alive. She held a baby blanket and cried. Lucas had said to him, "Your mother can't see you, but she loves you. If you climb on the bed, close your eyes and try to hold her; she will know you're there. She will stop crying. I promise." Toby didn't understand. He remembered trying to hold her as she wept. He couldn't figure out why he couldn't feel her. Toby could feel himself sinking as if becoming one with Lauren. It was as his father promised. Lauren stopped her tears and fell asleep. Lucas had tried to send Toby to the other side, but he didn't want to go. He wanted to be with Amanda. Toby had made his decision, not understanding his choice. He was to be a guide for his sister. They were bonded not only by blood but by spirit. Lucas didn't like it, but he had no option but to except it. Toby grew as

Amanda grew and changed, but it was by Amanda's will and design that he did so.

Toby was where he wanted to be. There was nothing else. Amanda was the only thing close to living for him. Even in death, their bond was strong. Sometimes he thought he could actually feel what she felt. As quickly as it came, it was gone. It was enough. It had to be. Toby's thoughts trailed back to the present. He knew she was inside the house. He stood in the foyer and listened. He could feel the others again. The whispering was louder, but he couldn't hear Amanda. His form was like a mist at the front of the stairs. He looked upward, looking for some sign that Amanda was all right. His form contorted when a presence walked through him. He was stunned for a moment.

The figure looked like Cheryl, but it wasn't Cheryl. She had the appearance of the possessed. Her eyes seemed distant and fierce. When she turned, it was as if she could see him as much as he could see her. Toby moved back when she tilted her head sinisterly and waved her index finger side to side, scolding him. Her smile unveiled a row of broken teeth and blood. With a loud tut, she moved back toward Toby, about to charge him, full force. She screamed, her hands guiding her on. Toby turned to the foot of the stairs when he heard Amanda. He disappeared to his new destination.

When he arrived, everything was black. He was amazed

at what he saw. Amanda was in his window shouting. When he heard a noise behind him, he turned to find himself in the middle of a nasty predicament. Marcus was in the far corner of the room. To his right was a mass of flesh. It walked toward the Shikoba boy on two legs. He could hear whispering from within the collection of muscle and bone. Toby didn't have a clue what he was seeing and had never seen anything like it. He didn't even know if there was anything human about it. His vision focused better in the darkness, taking in all the elements around his presence.

Marcus had seen Amanda had come back for him. He shook his head as a warning. Amanda did not heed his warning and continued inside.

"Amanda, what are you doing?"

My face was flushed as I moved in Marcus's direction. I ran through Toby and to where I had seen Marcus. I moved beside him, trying to get him to stand. I didn't want to look at it. I just wanted to get out. I turned around when I heard the scuffling behind me. It moved at a faster pace after it saw me. Marcus stood and moved against the wall with me, trying to stay clear of the thing. It reached out a hand to me, trying to touch me. Marcus moved forward, protecting me from the form. I couldn't see its face. The hooded apparition let out a terrifying wail as it tried to push Marcus aside. It was formed of many body parts and fallen flesh. As a gust of wind hit, the figure's hood moved to reveal a disfigured face of flesh and bones. The creature began to speak. I could hear it, but couldn't understand its words. The language was very foreign to me. Toby was behind it, unsure of what to do, but he knew what it wanted. Toby made an attempt to slow it down. Before it could get any closer, Toby make a noise, hoping it could hear him. It turned slightly to see the source of the sound.

"Amanda, run!"

I nodded and ran with Marcus to the window. The creature came for me. As it reached out, a large light flashed between us. The form stumbled backwards.

Marcus was reaching his hand out to me as he stood on the tree limb outside. The structure shook violently as we made our escape. I climbed through the window and ventured down the tree. As we climbed down, the house began to have a life of its own. I covered my ears with my hands as I heard the high-pitch scream that emanated from the inside. I took Marcus's hand in my own as we bolted to his motorcycle. He started the engine quickly, turned, and placed his helmet on my head.

"Hold on," he shouted as the tires spun beneath us, leaving a trail of dust behind.

I held tightly to his waist, afraid of losing my grip. I turned slightly to look at the old house. Its core shook violently as the shutters from the outside rapped loudly. I thought the house would soon implode. I held on tighter when I observed a dark black shadow begin to swallow up the home. By my tight grip, Marcus knew that it wasn't a good sign. He knew we couldn't stop, for if he did, whatever it was behind them would consume them. He continued in the darkness, looking for a way out.

I could see the shadow take on a life of its own. The menacing presence expressed its anger. It was like a cloud of black smoke that slithered through the trees with predatory-like movement. The sound it was making was frightening. It was a cloud of nothingness, an empty core of hate and vengeance. It was apparent that the house wasn't letting me go. It was quickly gaining on us. As it approached the motor bike, I could hear the screams. The sound was terrible. It sounded as though there were thousands within its hollow interior. It reminded me of the painful cries of the damned and dying. The feeling had plagued my mind with fear and questions. It was getting too close. We couldn't outrun it. I turned in Marcus's direction, not wanting to witness anymore.

I noticed the large gap in the distance. It looked as though the land had been swallowed up from beneath, leaving nothing but a blank space. I could feel pain in the pit of my stomach when Marcus screamed, "Hold on to me!"

The barrier was coming up so fast I didn't have time to hold my breath. The gorge was wide, but Marcus was determined and confident. As he increased speed, I stiffened up and closed my eyes. I felt it as we broke contact with the ground below and moved forward. Sometimes moments like these seem to last forever. It was like time stood still, leaving us with the anticipation of safe haven and freedom. I could feel Marcus's body stiffen, and I braced myself for the hard bump that we were about to encounter. When we made contact with the rugged edge, I could feel the bike kick back a bit before it continued on its course to our unknown destination. It felt like Marcus began to breathe again. He pivoted the bike sideways as the motorcycle came to an abrupt halt. We noticed that the cloud was gone, but it didn't feel right. Something else was coming.

Chapter 23

Grandfather Shikoba waited for Trent. He feared the evil of that land. None of his people would go there. It terrified him to go back to that place, but he was more afraid of losing his grandson. Trent never understood him or his ways, but Marcus did. He was so much like Grandfather Shikoba. He went to his shed and opened a burlap bag. He quickly screened all the contents of the room, trying to devise a plan. Nadie Shikoba couldn't stand waiting for Trent any longer. There were herbs and plants that stood before him. He chanted as he continued in meditation and contemplation. He placed his hands in a large bowl as he moved with his songs to the Great Spirit. As he pulled his hands from the bowl, he touched his face with open palms and applied the white powder. He began to eat the peyote as his chanting continued on. The inner calm began to build inside him as he breathing slowed down. The colors in the room became brighter and more defined. Clarity, calm, and serenity awaited him in the spirit world. He began to grab other herbs in plastic casing from the shelf as he asked the Great Spirit for the way. He opened a container that was filled with paints of different colors. With his index fingers he touched the green color.

With his middle fingers he touched the black. He placed his fingers beneath his eyes and followed the path of his cheekbones across his face. Shikoba closed his eyes and listened to his surroundings. He could see a vision, blurred at first, but as it came closer, the image became clear.

The guardian of the Great Spirit was a white horse. The creature pranced and raised his front hooves on the air, kicking in defiance and strength. He watched as it danced around him, assessing him. He fell to his knees in thankfulness and respect. "Guardian of the Great Spirit, show me. Show me the way."

He closed his eyes again, listening to the songs of his ancestors. The chorus of unseen voices became louder in the room. He nodded in understanding. The mustang came closer, so Nadie and the creature were eye to eye. He dared not touch the sacred animal before him. He feared breaking the connection.

"What must be done?" he yelled out as he chanted.

The horse remained silent. There were no words necessary between them. It bobbed its head up and down as its mane swayed violently. It started to turn away, unveiling the brilliant colors of red palm prints on its white coat. It whinnied loudly, giving out its command.

"If it is your will, it shall be," Nadie shouted. The wind picked up wildly as a bright light appeared behind the grand creature. It stomped its feet speaking in his own language. The brightness of the light was too much for the old warrior. He turned his head slightly and covered his brow with the palm of his hand. With one last glance, Nadie watched as the light opened a door of what was to be. It was quick and brief, but the message was clear. Nadie knew what he had to do. The messenger bobbed its head once again and then it was engulfed by the light and disappeared.

Grandfather Shikoba was startled when Trent opened the large door. He stared at his father as if he had seen a ghost. Bringing his initial reaction back in check, he asked, "What are you doing?" Lauren poked her head out from behind Trent's back, curious.

Nadie threw the bag at his son's chest in disgust. "We must go to the house. Marcus is there."

Trent rolled his eyes up to the heavens and prayed for patience. He paused for a brief second before asking, "How do you know where Marcus is?"

Nadie was becoming impatient. "Because I know."

Trent just nodded in acknowledgment. By his father's questioning look, Trent answered before he could ask. "Amanda's mother." Trent gave out the information in his native tongue.

Grandfather Shikoba nodded in acceptance then started to move toward the car. "I am surprised you remember our language," Grandfather Shikoba said in Choctaw.

Before Trent could say another word to his father, Nadie opened and closed the door. Trent quickly dug his hands in his pockets to retrieve the key to the car. He pulled the door of the car forcefully and then shut it soundly for effect. Trent turned the key in the ignition, starting the vehicle. Lauren rushed in before he could place the car in gear. Trent saw Derek at the side of his window, tapping the glass with his key.

Trent rolled down his window in frustration. "Derek, I didn't see you. Is there a problem?"

Derek frowned slightly. "No problem. I just figured I would stop by to talk to your dad for a minute."

"Can't it wait, Derek? I am trying to find my son and Amanda right now."

Derek placed his hood on his head when it started to rain. "I guess it could wait for a little while. Where you off to?"

"Lauren's house."

Derek smiled. "Sure thing. Tell you what. I'll follow you out there and give you guys a hand."

Trent looked down and nodded. "All right, Derek."

Trent rolled up the window and looked back at his father in disgust. "What did you do this time, old man?"

"We need to get to that house, Trent." That was all Nadie said.

Lauren agreed. "I must admit I am eager to get home. I hope the kids are there." Lauren shivered slightly.

During the ride, Grandfather spoke in his language. "Whether you would like to admit it or not, you and Marcus are alike in many ways."

Trent didn't comment.

Grandfather looked down at his feet in defeat. "I think it is that very reason that you two do not get along."

When Grandfather Shikoba got the hint that Trent didn't want to talk, he began to dwell on his thoughts. He had gone to the house long before to try to warn the family before the Pennington's, but they did not listen or understand. He gazed down at the palms of his hands, questioning. He knew what had to be done. Trent wouldn't understand or forgive for what he was about to do. He could only hope that someday he would understand. His dark eyes made contact with his son's briefly, and then Trent quickly led his eyes away. Maybe Grandfather Shikoba was not the best of fathers, but he always did the right thing. He knew that Trent felt neglected and unappreciated, but Nadie did love his son. He just wished he could see that. The only thing that Nadie couldn't understand was why Trent couldn't see that he was doing the same thing to his own son that Nadie had done to Trent. Nadie gazed at the window and stared at his reflection. The image seemed like a stranger of an unspoken truth. One thing was clear. He may have failed his son, but he wouldn't fail his grandson. Nadie looked back up into Trent's rearview mirror. Nadie's last thoughts centered on his son. He hoped that Trent would forgive the decision he had made for himself tonight. He could only hope that he would understand, for the meaning of seeing the Guardian of the Great Spirit signified death.

Chapter 24

It was as if time moved in slow motion. I noticed the clearing before us and an old tree that was withered and old. I thought I heard the sound of a train in the distance that became louder as the seconds past. I took the helmet off my head so I could see better, but it didn't help. Marcus kept his hands on the handles as I clasped mine against my ears. The wind gusted forth with such force that the dirt and leaves kicked up into our eyes. The ground around us steamed with heat that was emanating from the depths below. I couldn't explain what was causing it, but Marcus didn't dwell on it for long. He turned the motor bike around, trying to judge the distance across, knowing full well that he couldn't make the jump back. The space between where we were and the gorge wouldn't be enough space to gain enough momentum, and he knew it. He placed his head down, defeated, and gazed back at the clearing with a small ravine before them. His thoughts forbade him to continue forward, but forward was the only way out. I could tell from the look in his eyes where his thoughts were going. With unsteady hands, I placed the helmet on him and nodded in agreement. He turned the throttle, revving the engine.

I placed my head on his back and whispered, "I trust you."

He continued, gaining speed as I again tightened my grip around his midsection. I didn't think it was easy. I knew something was coming. I could feel it in every bone in my body. I did something I hadn't done in years. I actually prayed. I prayed with every part of my being. I felt my stomach drop as we lost ground. We went into a free fall. It seemed like an eternity until I felt us hit soil. It was then that I felt the second wave. It was a rush of force that kicked the motorcycle from under us, sending Marcus and me tumbling on the grassy knoll. Marcus held me in his arms, taking the brunt of the fall as we tumbled downward. I couldn't get my thoughts in order.

How can a person have a normal life one moment and then in the next instant be surrounded by complete and utter chaos? I grunted in pain with every blow from the ground. When we stopped falling, Marcus looked up at me in a daze and agony. In the midst of the fall, the bike had tumbled with us, pinning his leg. I knelt down beside him, trying to release him from the hold of the tire. He couldn't get out from under it. The more I tried to free him, the more hopeless a task it came to be. I turned the bike off. When he was finally free, I could see that his leg was broken. Marcus gritted his teeth in pain as he held his leg. I tried to get on the bike and start it, but it was no use. It wouldn't start. I looked down at Marcus. I knew there was no way that Marcus could walk. The bike was our only chance for escape. It was then that I could hear a whisper in the distance. It was a voice that beckoned me to come. The wind seemed to softly speak out to me.

Marcus shouted at me and then took my hand to get my attention. "Run, Amanda. Run."

I didn't move. I couldn't leave him like that. I knew that if I ran, Marcus wouldn't make it. With all the courage within myself, I stood up, released my grip from Marcus's, and began to move forward toward the old tree that spoke out my name. Marcus tried to reach out to detain me, but by that time I was too far away from his grasp. This gift that I had, I didn't understand or want.

"Amanda."

I couldn't look back. I continued to move toward the tree. After a few steps, it became easier to move. I could still feel the heat rise from beneath my feet. The ground on the hilltop heaved and then released, as if it had a life of its own. I didn't know why I did what I did. It was like I had no control of my own movements. I walked closer to the tree and then I placed my open palms on it and closed my eyes. I felt something wet. When I released my hold, I looked upward, trying to see what was on my hands. The sticky substance was slick at first. As I raised my hands closer to my eyes, it became clear what it was, blood. My lips trembled as I backed away slowly. I had control of my movement again.

"Toby," I called out. At my call, the bark of the tree cracked in random places. I stepped back yet again.

The tree pulsated more as the bark fell to the ground. I took another step.

"Toby?"

I looked around, but Toby was not there. As I tried to move again, a hand quickly appeared from the center of the tree and took hold of me, pulling me closer. The coarse palms held my throat as it raised my body higher. My feet dangled and kicked as I fought to breathe. I tried to free myself. My hands were much smaller than his. It was no use. I couldn't win. I tried to speak, but no words followed. I tried to breathe, but it was no use. I was losing consciousness quickly. Just before I gave in to the darkness, the hand released me. I fell onto the ground.

My lungs burned as I took in my first breath. The explosion of air made me dizzy. I couldn't catch my breath. It was as if my body continued to greedily take in air. I raised my eyes to see none other than my Great Nanny who stood before me. She was a wonderful sight to behold.

"Can you walk?" she shouted.

I rose as quickly as I could to get out of the situation. Ivy's attention was back on the tree. I couldn't talk. I held my throat, trying to express my thanks.

"Let's go, lady," she said with great insistence.

"Marcus," was all I could say.

"The boy is fine. He's safe. I can't say as much for us."

As I looked up, Ivy's mother and Toby were next to each other. They were all talking at once. I couldn't understand what they were saying, but I knew what they wanted. I stood up and staggered. Ivy held my arm. "If you don't get your bum moving, lady, you'll kill us both."

I looked up at the sinister apparition. It was a man clothed in deerskins. In shear surprise, I rubbed my neck again. I tried again, but my feet couldn't gain control. I couldn't feel them. My breathing was still shallow. It didn't take long for the unknown specter to be freed from his prison. He moved closer to us and held out his hand. Nanny Ivy's mother appeared and pushed, making the creature stumble backwards a bit.

"Get that grandchild of ours up and moving."

"I thought you couldn't interfere, Mam," I heard Ivy ask.

"I can only do so much," Ivy's mother said with impatience.

My feet finally obeyed and we began to move away. We fell again as the ground shook beneath us. Ivy placed her hands in her pockets and threw something over her shoulder. As the granules touched the ominous vision, it staggered as if burned.

"Sea salt," she shouted over the scream. "It burns them."

It slowed him down but only temporarily. It seemed to anger the creature more than anything. Its appearance changed quickly; it was now neither man nor beast. The creature swayed and staggered like a burning flame. I heard the apparition scream some word in another language as he plunged his hands into the ground below.

Lauren and Trent had pulled into the driveway with Derek not far behind them. Grandfather Shikoba opened the door and got out of the vehicle quickly, not wasting any time. He stared at the house briefly and then looked around in a state of panic.

"House hollow shell. Marcus not here."

Trent stared at his father with disgust. He placed his hand over his face, praying for patience. "Stop it, Dad. Just stop. It's just a house, nothing more," Trent enunciated every word showing his disapproval. Trent took a deep breath and dropped his hands to his sides. "Let's just go in the house and see if the kids are there."

"Not there," Grandfather replied. "You go." He pointed toward the house.

Lauren opened the front door and called out Amanda's name in desperation. She walked inside looking for her daughter.

Trent turned in his dad's direction, exasperated. He watched as his father disappeared into the woods. "I'll get him."

Lauren placed her hand on Trent's shoulder. "I'll go with you. No one's here."

Derek crossed his arms. "I think we should all go."

Lauren and Trent both raised their eyes to Derek one more time as they walked down the porch stairs and began their journey into the woods.

Chapter 25

Marcus tried to move his leg, but it was of no use. It was broken. He could feel the bone shift that was protruding outside his skin as he tried to stand up. Marcus fell hard, holding his right leg as he cried out. He rolled to his side to see what was happening. He couldn't see anything, but he could hear. He crawled toward the source of the sound. In a panicked frenzy, he moved to his bike. Pushing it up, he got on and made an attempt to start the engine. He continued to yell at the motorcycle in anger and fright. He turned the key, yet the bike would not start. Marcus punched the tank, as if his effort would make the engine start. He rolled his eyes upward and asked for help. He turned the key again. When he heard the sweet sound of the engine, it was music to his ears. He revved the engine to get a good start for what he had in mind. He wiped the blood that was dripping down his face as he picked his feet up off the ground, driving toward his target.

Toby tried to hold me back as the creature reached out. Marcus rushed past us on his bike and then jumped off it before it collided with its target. The creature flew backwards when the motorcycle made contact.

"Bloody Hell!" Nan Ivy whispered a quick prayer of

thanks and placed her arm around me. Ivy looked down at Marcus. "Marcus, can you walk?" Nanny shouted in a hopeful tone.

Marcus stood up. "I can try."

"Mam?" Ivy looked up at her mother hopelessly. "It looks like I'll be joining you sooner than expected."

"I'll do what I can, Ivy." Ivy's mother nodded her head in Toby's direction as a signal. "I am going to need you, Toby."

Toby didn't like the sound of it, but he was willing to do what he could. "All right."

Toby took the hand of his great-great-grandmother, and as he did, a bright light formed around them. "Ivy, you need to go," the old woman said.

Ivy knew what her mother was doing and knew fair well that she may never see her again. "Mam, there has to be another way."

Abby shook her head negatively. "I need Toby's energy. You better get going. It will only stun him a bit, but it will give you some time. You have to go."

Ivy knew that by her mother's interference, she would disappear and in turn be shifted from this plane.

"Mam, you can't do this."

"It must be done love. Good-bye." With Abby's last word, she turned back to the Witiko.

"I love you, Mam."

"It's all right; he will be drawn to our light," Abby

whispered. "It will be all right."

Ivy could hear Ahote's anger and pain. He moved forward toward the light. The bright luminous light became brighter. The beam was the energy that kept Toby and Abby on this plane. The creature was drawn to it like a magnet to metal. It felt the pull and tried to resist it. Toby was giving his great nanny all the power he could muster. The Witiko couldn't slow his speed down. They finally reached each other. The Witiko's body retracted quickly; he lay silently on the ground. The light fragmented into a thousand pieces, leaving nothing but smoke and dust.

We retreated into the woods for refuge. Ivy watched in the woods as her mother disappeared. She looked up in sadness as a tear slowly traced the contours of her face. Ivy knew her mother was gone. She knew of the sacrifice that she had given her. It was, however, short lived. Ivy heard a sound that made her look back out into the clearing.

The creature was still there. Abby's sacrifice didn't give them the time that they needed. The Witiko began to change again. "Amanda, we need to get out of here now," Ivy said in a panic.

The Witiko's body began to convulse as he fell down on all fours. All of its teeth became jagged as it opened its mouth. The smooth olive complexion turned into a gray, rubbery hide. Horns began to pierce through the skin of the beast as his hands and feet became talons. It looked up sinisterly, trying to locate its prey. It didn't take too long to find our destination. It stopped suddenly and opened its eyes. The Witiko stared in our direction and moved forward in large strides. Nanny Ivy looked toward Marcus and me. I held Marcus in my arms. With one hand placed gently on his right ear, I said, "We've got to go."

Ivy and I stood as we both tried to help Marcus. He grunted softly when he tried to walk. "It's no use, Amanda. Leave me here. I am just slowing you down."

I shook my head in defiance.

"Listen to me. Get out of here and get help. I'll keep it busy."

I remained where I was, and I knelt down beside him. "I am staying right here."

Marcus pushed me away. "Get out of here. Now," he shouted.

Before I could say another word, my Nanny grabbed me from behind and began to pull me away. "We have to go now, Amanda. Without mam's help, I can't do anything." The wind picked up like a slow-moving cyclone. Nanny's hair came undone, leaving a wild mess of white that moved violently around her.

"I can't leave," I said defiantly.

Nanny Ivy turned to find the dark monster close. She stuffed her hands in the pockets of Dad's overcoat and threw the salt again and then ordered the creature not to take another step. I did not know how or when she had obtained Dad's coat, but in a way, it suited her. Nanny knelt down and pulled out a book and began speaking in another language. Ahote seemed stunned and faltered a bit. I watched as she raised her hands to the sky, calling upon unseen forces. Her large bracelets moved with her as she waved her hands back and forth. Ivy looked like the stereotypical gypsy. Her brightly colored attire flared with her as the winds continued to kick up. The lightning flashed and the rains came down. I knelt down by Marcus and held onto him, fearing I would be blown away from the powerful change in the weather.

It was terrifying to see this creature in its true form. I remembered Nita and the story that Grandfather Shikoba told. I shouted out her name, thinking she would hear me and help, but nothing happened. Ahote was not pleased. I could tell by its body language. The creature tried to step in my direction. Ivy wouldn't allow it. She shouted out another word that made it turn at her. It was close to Ivy, but she didn't move from her spot. Its doglike face smiled, showing its fanged teeth, implying what would happen if she continued.

Nanny began to look scared.

"Oh dear."

It took another step. It loomed over Ivy, showing its act of victory. She smoothed her wild hair back a bit to make eye contact and then calmly stated, "What do you suggest now, lovey? Perhaps a game of bridge?" She smiled sarcastically as the creature bellowed out a horrid sound.

I screamed as I watched Ahote's arm move back, and in one swift motion, he knocked Nanny aside.

"No! Nan!"

It came closer to me.

Before I knew it, the creature was right in front of me, smelling my clothing and deeply taking in the scent.

Marcus was sitting up when he said, "Go to hell."

Its eyes moved to him as it licked its teeth with its serpent-like tongue. It started to bring its talons forward to grab Marcus. I screamed again as it pulled him up by his shirt front and held him. Marcus's feet dangled from the ground. I got up and tried to push the creature away. It was no use. It didn't even budge. The Witiko bit down onto Marcus's shoulder, savoring the taste of him. The rush filled its senses to new heights as it continued to feed. Marcus stuck his hand in his own pants pocket and pulled out his house key. In one swift motion, he swung his arm upward, digging the metal into the left eye of the Witiko. The creature swayed its antlers side to side as it screamed out in pain. Marcus was dropped, and he rolled to avoid being crushed by the creature's stomping feet. I ran to Marcus's side when the creature regained its composure. It then came back, straight for Marcus.

"No!" I screamed out.

It stopped midway toward its prey.

"Stop," I whispered. It looked at me. "Please stop."

The creature's belly shook as a sound escaped its

mouth. It sounded like uncontrolled laughter. It slowly moved my way, sizing up me up. I could see in its eyes. We were strangely connected. I could feel its heartbeat quicken in anticipation. I could hear it breathe. I could see a face of anger and pain. I could hear its promise of revenge. For that one single moment, I actually felt pity for the creature. To want, need, love, and then to lose it suddenly was sad. In a way I understood how the creature felt. Even evil can love. It seemed as though it understood what I was doing. I wanted it to feel my pain and fear. I knew it understood, but it didn't want to listen.

Ivy dusted her skirts in a fuss and got herself back to rights. "Why that bloody bugger!" Ivy looked out to see what was happening. When her faculties were all back in order, she realized what I was doing. She didn't like it. "No, Amanda," she screamed out. "Don't!"

The tips of its talons touched my finger tips. I felt it. I saw what it had seen, felt what it had felt. Everything became clear. It didn't want to talk or stop. It just wanted to eat. Little did I know that there were many ways the creature fed. It finally occurred to me, it didn't want anyone else. It was always about me. It wanted whatever it was I had. It could feel the energy that came from within me. I could feel the Witiko take it away. It started like a tingle at first, and then it became painful. It was taking not only my gift of sight but my life force. It gave me a piece of itself before it could take the energy inside me. Images continued to flash within my mind. I fell to my knees in pain and delirium. When I opened my eyes, I could no longer see what was going on around me. I could only see the past. I could feel it seeping inside, taking whatever it could. Its greedy lust for energy continued its conquest, draining me of everything. I thought I heard a sound like a distant echo. It sounded like Marcus's grandfather calling out.

"Issa, Ahote!"

I felt the creature break contact with me. When its hand left mine, I fell to the ground and lay there, unable to move. I opened my eyes to see Grandfather Shikoba dressed like his ancestors. His face was colorful and brightly painted. The proud warrior never faltered as he moved forward. I tried to raise my hands slowly out to him. My right arm shook as I tried to keep it high above me. Instead I felt another hand entwined in mine. It was Marcus's. I noticed his lips were moving, but I couldn't hear him. Nanny Ivy appeared also and helped Marcus lift me from the cold ground onto his lap in a sitting position. I felt my body go into convulsions as I tried to remain focused and awake. I heard Toby, but he seemed far away, and then there was nothing.

Chapter 26

Derek was lost. He tried to chase Lauren and Trent. He stopped and leaned against a tree to catch his breath. The path before him forked in two different directions. "Trent!" There was no response, just silence.

"Lauren," he said more softly.

A snapping of a twig brought his attention to the darkness behind him. He released his gun from its holster and waited beside the tree, wondering if he should investigate. It was so cold that his breath misted as exhaled. His breathing was a bit off, for he was still out of breath from the run through the thick woods. He cursed himself for not bringing a flashlight, but Derek didn't intend to run in the dark of night. He pulled out his gun and pointed it, waiting for another sound.

"Hello, Trent, is that you? Show yourself!"

Silence.

"This is Officer Felding, EPD. Come out!"

Derek felt a surge of wind that swept through the dense woods. He never felt a gust that hard. The violence of it almost made him fall over. The wind did not distract him from the sound behind him. He spun around, confused of where the noise was coming from. It sounded like whispering, but it was everywhere. Derek couldn't tell exactly where the source was. The whispering was becoming so loud that it seemed to echo in his head. The voices continued to speak faster and faster. He couldn't understand what the voices were saying. Derek wanted to shout, but the voices were so loud that it felt as though his head would explode into a million pieces. His hands were pressed over his ears, in an attempt to block out the noise. It wasn't working. He couldn't escape the sounds.

"Stop! Stop! Stop it!" he shouted.

Blood began to drip from Derek's nose, mouth and ears. He coughed, trying to dislodge the clots of blood that blocked his esophagus. He fell down on his knees in agony and rolled to his side. He remained in the fetal position until the noise ceased suddenly.

Derek removed his hands from his ears when he was certain that it was over. His breathing began to slow. He looked around, confused and relieved at the same time. He stood up and quickly spit out the remains of blood that was inside his mouth. He wiped the blood from the sides of his ears. He stared down, baffled by what just transpired. He attempted to remove the blood from his hands, wiping them across his pants. He placed the weapon back in its holster when he thought he was safe.

"What the hell was that?"

Derek spit one more time, letting out what was left of the blood. When he heard a noise in the trees, he couldn't turn quickly enough. The hissing sound threw him off-guard as something jumped into his line of vision. The object hit his chest, and he fell over. He touched his front to make sure everything was still there as he turned to find the source of his scare.

His eyes adjusted in the dark area. Around the tree he noticed a small tan furry animal approach him.

The Siamese cat looked at the officer with curiosity. Derek laughed out loud for his moment of fright. He chuckled louder as the cat meowed and came closer to him.

"Where did you come from, you little runt?" The cat purred loudly when she was in Derek's arms.

"Are you hurt, buddy?" Derek could see the blood on the animal's coat but could not find any puncture wounds on the animal. The poor thing looked like it had been through hell. The fact that it wasn't the cat's blood alarmed Derek. He knew that the blood wasn't from a small critter. It had to have come from something bigger.

"What's your name?" Derek eyed the cat's name tag and turned it over so he could read the name.

"Taboo, huh?"

Derek became more alarmed when he saw the address on the tag of the animal. It had 210 Water Street engraved in it. Derek stroked the animal, knowing full well that someone was hurt.

"Where did you come from?"

Taboo began to growl and hiss as the ground rumbled beneath them. Derek lost his grip on the cat. Derek tried to keep his footing as he walked in the opposite direction from where the feline went. Wherever the cat had been, there was someone injured. Derek just knew it.

Grandfather Shikoba hoped he wasn't too late. He waved his hands from side to side. "The time for your people is gone. You must move on. The Great Spirit knows this. He is sad for you brother."

Ahote seethed with anger and hate. "We cannot change what we are, Nadie."

Grandfather Shikoba nodded. "No, we cannot, but we can change what we become."

"Then it begins," Ahote shouted as he charged the old warrior.

Grandfather Shikoba slammed his staff soundly onto the ground as he chanted to his ancestors for help and guidance. It felt as though the whole world were shaking. The ground moved with violence and spoke of redemption of the past. A mist arose and began to take form. Ahote stopped and watched to see what the old man had brought forth. As the image became clearer, Ahote was taken aback with surprise. It was a woman from one of the nations. Ahote could never forget the woman he once loved and lost in this madness. Nita stared at him with a look of disapproval and fear. Ahote began to charge again, not liking the trick of the conjurer. Nita placed her hands in front of her, pleading him, but he continued forward without hesitation. The creature didn't stop until he was face to face with her.

"It is time to let go of this world, Ahote. Leave these souls alone and leave the others at peace," Nita pleaded.

Ahote's appearance changed to that of the man he once was. He didn't want Nita to see him as a beast. "I would want nothing more than to be with you, Nita. You know that will never be." He touched her hand. It was something he had longed to do. It had been too long since he had touched her in the physical world.

"I cannot move on, Ahote. The death on this land has plagued my soul. My people did what they thought was right." Nita's tears began to fall.

Ahote stared at her intensely. "To sacrifice someone for their own lives wasn't the right thing. I believe after a few hundred years of punishment, they have realized that."

"The children, Ahote; I still hear their cries. It must end."

"It shall be as it has been. We will both be prisoners here for all eternity." Ahote embraced Nita and held her tight. "I am sorry, Nita; now that I have you, I can't let go. It will be as I wanted it. Together, you and me, as one forever."

Nita fought the hold the man had her in, but it was

no use. She was losing form and began to dissipate. As the vapor reappeared, so did the fading of the woman's image. Ahote didn't let her escape. He took in the entire miasma within himself. The smoke and ash entered through the skin of Ahote's body. He smiled at first like he was content and happy, but it was short lived. He opened his eyes and pinned them on Grandfather Shikoba.

"We are creatures of habit, Nadie. Let us finish what has begun, for I will never stop. Not even for her."

Grandfather Shikoba shook his staff forcefully as Ahote charged him. Ahote slowly began changing back into his animal-like form. Grandfather Shikoba remained steadfast. He waited for the creature. When it was close enough, Nadie brought the staff forward toward the creature. Grandfather Shikoba plunged the sharp end of his walking stick into the chest of the beast.

Ahote screamed as he stood up and pulled out the staff. Ahote pushed the warrior with such force that Grandfather fell, hitting his head.

Trent and Lauren were not far behind. When Trent hit the clearing, he saw his father being attacked. Trent ran in Grandfather Shikoba's direction, and my mother ran to me.

Trent didn't know what it was that stood before him. It was then the creature spoke in his native tongue.

"You should not have abandoned your people. You cannot help your father now."

Ahote bared its teeth as it came forward for the attack. The flash and sound of a gunshot fired behind them. The Witiko flinched from the impact of the bullet and then turned to see Derek with unsteady hands. The evidence of smoke rose above the pistol. The creature was distracted, but only for a moment. That was all Nadie Shikoba needed. Grandfather rose and drove his staff into the creature again from behind. This time it had found its target. The force of the impalement was so strong that the staff pierced completely through. Ahote knew what the old man was up to, but the Witiko wanted to make sure that he wouldn't finish. As the Nadie opened his bag, the Witiko grabbed him and pulled Nadie to him, plunging the stick into Grandfather Shikoba also.

"Dad!" Trent screamed.

Grandfather's facial expression changed from triumph to pain. He knew this was to come, but he wasn't finished with the ritual. He still held his bag of herbs tightly in his hand.

"You have failed like the others, Nadie."

Grandfather smiled as he dumped the herbs over the creature and himself. Grandfather Shikoba coughed out loud, trying to inhale, but oxygen wasn't filling his lungs. He let out his last breath, knowing that he had failed.

The creature pulled Grandfather Shikoba's lifeless body from him and threw him down. Trent took his father and held him close. He could hear Marcus in the distance yelling out. Trent shook as he shouted in remorse. He kept shaking his father, looking for some sign of life.

It was then that I woke up, overcoming the darkness. Toby was above me. His eyes were gazing into mine.

I didn't know what was happening or where it came from. Toby stood beside me as I rose and walked slowly over to Trent. I knew my mother was yelling out to me, but I continued to walk forward. Toby took my hand in his and nodded as I approached the Witiko. I didn't know what to do. I didn't even know what force pulled me closer to the evil. It held out its hand to me and moved it fingertips up and down, bidding me to come closer to him. I went into its embrace as I heard my mother scream. Its eyes blazed yellow as I continued to walk into the cradle of its arms. Ahote was pleased. I held on tight as I heard Ahote scream in agony.

I continued to hold onto it as it slashed its body around. I knew that I had to finish what Grandfather Shikoba started. I stepped back holding the fetish in my palms, taking in the evil energy. The bear effigy glowed as the Witiko fought. The more it resisted, the more painful the process was for the beast. The animal was not ready to go so easily.

The Witiko was too close. He came into possession of the fetish and crushed it in its palms. The Witiko was a man again and couldn't change back into his creature-like form. In anger Ahote took his hand and slapped me, making his mark across my cheek. As my body hit the soft earth, I felt my mother and Nanny came to my side.

Toby was powerless; he didn't have enough energy to help us. He had given what power he had to Abby.

The creature that was now man had had enough. He decided it was time to end this. It was me he had in his sights. We were powerless. There was nothing we could do now. I tried to push my family aside as I made my stand.

Taboo appeared, jumping between the Witiko and me. The Siamese gave a loud hiss. Taboo turned, leaping into my arms. The animal growled again, warning Ahote, but he continued to move closer to me. As he came forward to touch me, the cat struck his hand with a swipe of its claws. The cut of the feline's nails dug deep into the hand of Ahote, leaving a large mark. It was then that it happened. An explosion erupted from behind us. The bright blues and red fluorescents filled the air around me. The lights followed Taboo as the animal pounced on Ahote. I could hear the whispering surrounding me, but the words were inaudible. Toby's facial expression changed to that of astonishment. Ahote grabbed for me again. In that instant a light flashed brightly behind him.

It took a moment for our eyes to adjust. I stared in wonder and happiness when we could see what was in the luminous haze. "Dad," I whispered.

"Lucas," Mother shouted.

My father's arms encased the entity and pulled him back. Into the ground they plundered as the mouth of the land opened up. Mother Earth's greedy need was ready to receive the creature openly. They continued deep into the bowels below. The Witiko yelled out in anger as he tried to scale back up into our world. The last thing we saw was the fingertips of thousands of souls that held the creature at bay. It was then that Dad took one last look at us. I could see the hurt and sorrow in his eyes. He opened his mouth to say something, but I couldn't hear him, and then they were gone. They were all gone. I stood up with my family.

"Dad," I whispered. "Dad!"

It all happened so quickly. My mind was still putting together all the pieces of what had just transpired. Like a floodgate, my emotions took control in the aftermath. So many different emotions—fear, grief, pain, relief, and guilt were all rolled into one. I tried to dry the tears from my face, but they were quickly replaced with more tears.

Lauren placed her hands on her mouth as she staggered to the site were my father made his appearance. She knelt down in shock and denial as she caressed the grass and grabbed some of the blades in her hands. "Lucas."

Ivy held onto my mother. Mom cried a thousand tears that she swore she would never shed again.

Marcus, Trent, and Derek crowded around Grandfather Shikoba, looking down at his lifeless body. I was torn. I just stood where I was, in grief, with only Toby and Taboo by my side.

Epilogue

I couldn't stop thinking of what Marcus had said to me that night. The flashing of the lights of the emergency medical unit entranced me. EMS was taking Marcus, and Trent was waiting inside the vehicle. Marcus turned one last time to watch the gurney that held the remains of his grandfather being taken away. I held him, hoping that my warmth would help the coldness that seeped within him. His grief broke my heart, and there was nothing I could do to make the hurt go away. Grandfather Shikoba had such an impact in Marcus's life. I felt like everything was my fault. I could only hope Marcus would forgive me one day. If I hadn't moved here to this house, this would have never happened. The heavy weight burdened my soul. I tried to block all the horrible images, but they still haunted me. Marcus held me tightly in his embrace.

As I looked out, I could see Officer Felding talking to fellow police officers about the incident. I couldn't even imagine what he had told them. Who would believe him? I was sure he was making something up. It was then that I caught sight of the covered body of Cheryl. The rest of the images that followed were in slower motion.

I watched as Cheryl disappeared into a coroner's van.

She was a lot of things, but she didn't deserve death. I closed my eyes, wishing the vision would leave me. My emotions remained in check as I continued to hold Marcus. We approached the opening of the ambulance together. Marcus wanted me to stay. Trent nodded his approval to the EMS. I sat across from Trent as the paramedics raised Marcus into the EMS transport. The doors closed soundly in front of us, and the emergency vehicle began to move away from 210 Water Street.

Marcus called me over and beckoned me closer to him. As Marcus looked up at me, he held my face. "*Chi hollo li*, Amanda."

A few days later, we went to the funeral of Grandfather Shikoba. The tribal elders danced in their painted attire, celebrating the life of a great man. I watched as they placed the last stone over him in the cave of creation. I couldn't bear the pain anymore. I quickly closed my eyes, wishing to see something else, pushing away all the sorrowful thoughts. In the end I stood alone in front of Grandfather Shikoba's home. I could hear the chirping of the birds, and then an eerie silence crept into the scene, leaving me helpless and alone.

I heard a voice.

I awoke with a start to find someone sitting on the edge of bed, staring at me in silence. Taboo was there also, looking at me with a slight tilt of her head. When I realized it was my father at the foot of my bed, I wiped the perspiration from my face and leaned forward, embracing him quickly.

"I never thought I would see you again." I expressed myself with deep emotion.

I heard a slight chuckle and then a sigh. "I had to come back to say good-bye. Especially to you."

I released my hold on him to gaze at his face in question.

"Bad dream?" he asked knowingly.

I let out a slight sigh of frustration. "Yes and no. I was dreaming about that night at the clearing and Grandfather Shikoba."

He nodded in understanding.

"It's all my fault."

"No, Amanda," he stated with certainty. "It wasn't. It was meant to happen. Time will heal all wounds."

"Marcus said something to me that night."

Dad smiled.

"Do you know what he said to me?"

He moved his head up and down.

"Can you tell me what?"

Dad cut me off. "That is for Marcus to tell you. You should ask him, if you're so curious."

"I suppose." I waited a moment before I added, "I am afraid of the answer."

"You believe he blames you?"

"Wouldn't you?" I asked sarcastically. "I haven't seen him since Grandfather Shikoba's burial."

"Give him some time, Amanda. The boy lost someone very important to him. You understand."

"I hope you are right," I hugged him again. "At least you are back and I have you."

I released my hold from him when I heard his reply.

"You will not see me again, Amanda. It is time for me to go."

I began to cry. That was not the response that I expected. "All this time, and you never——"

"I was always here, Amanda. I never left. You just weren't paying attention. It was a whisper, a feeling, or a chill." He touched my arm, racking my body with a sense of cold. "I believe you have felt that a lot since you have lived here. I was here, just on a different plane. You always had Toby." He shrugged and then said, "Your mother had no one. I was always with your mother. She needed me the most. I couldn't leave. Not yet, till I knew she would be all right and you were safe."

I wiped a tear from my eye. "The way Trent Shikoba looks at her, I don't think she's lonely anymore."

Dad frowned. "Don't remind me."

As I thought about that night, I stared at my father in wonder. "You, you were the one I thought of when the fetish was destroyed."

Lucas nodded. "You called me, and the fetish brought

me to you."

I was caught up in some emotion. I didn't know what else to say. It dawned on me. "It was you, wasn't it? You were the reason Toby and I escaped the house. You were the light."

Dad touched my forehead, and before I knew it, images flashed and overcame me, engrossing my senses and mind. It was so much, so fast, yet I remembered every one of them. I had many memories of my father, ones I never knew I had. I looked at my father in confusion and awe.

"These are for you. They are my memories of us and our short time together through my eyes," he said, while pointing to his eyes for effect. "I believe I owe you that much for taking a better life away from you. It is a part of me you will always have. It will be something we both share. You will need it, for you also share a part of the Witiko. It was never the creature's intentions for you to survive." My father gave a distant look out the window as if his mind were wandering away.

I had so many questions that I didn't know where to start. "Will you ever come back?"

He shook his head again.

"Why?"

"I think we both know the answer to that. I am moving on, Amanda. I have to. I don't have a choice. Even in death, we souls have to watch how much we intervene with humanity." He looked at me again sadly. "There are costs for every action."

"You have to go because of me," I said, feeling a huge loss.

My father raised my head by placing his index finger underneath my chin. "It's because of you that I can move on. I was not in a good place, Amanda. I couldn't let anything happen to my family. I found the courage within myself to help, and by doing so, I have earned my place to where I was meant to be."

"I don't understand you, Dad. You are talking in riddles."

Dad laughed out loud. "You will understand better when your time comes. But that," he stated, shaking his finger at me, "won't be for some time."

I knew he was running out of time, so I hugged him tightly, afraid that if I let go, he would disappear. He cradled my head in his arms. "I am so sorry, baby. My time is almost up."

"Mom saw you. It was only for a moment, but she did."

"It was time for her to see the truth, especially now." Dad's mannerism changed and became serious. "I need you to listen to me, Amanda. I need you not to argue and do as I ask. It is important that you go to England to be with your Nanny for a while." He held my face in his hands to look at the expression on my face.

"Why?" I asked, puzzled.

"This thing that you and I have. This..." he hesitated

to find the right word. "This gift needs to be controlled." He nodded with certainty. "I never wanted this for you, Amanda, but there is nothing that can be done about it. There are things about our abilities that can change you, and it's not for the better. Your Nan understands this and knows what she needs to do. That is why she is coming to get you, and you need to make your mother understand that you have to go. You must tell her this is what I want her to do for you. Now that she has seen for herself, she will believe you, but she won't let you go without a fight."

I nodded in agreement.

Dad inhaled again. "I don't want to go. There is so much you need to know, but Mum will do what I can't. There are other elements out there like what you have seen. There is good all around, but with the good there is bad. The other night something was left within you from the Witiko. It scares me to know that you will be here with that evil inside you." He stood up and stared down at me. "The box. The box that I had shown you. There is something in there for you. It is something that you will need. You will be seventeen soon." He seemed desperate, like he was running out of time. "On your seventeenth birthday, you will notice changes within you. You will do things you wouldn't normally do. You have to maintain control. Listen to your conscience."

"I don't understand."

"There are other things that you are not capable of yet.

When it happens, you must maintain focus and hold back. For some reason, the women are stronger in their abilities than men in our circles. The change is more intense for you. Your Nanny will prepare you for that day."

I stood up, and he began to slowly fade away.

"Dad, please don't leave me." I reached out for him.

"Bye, Amanda."

I could hear the sadness in his voice.

"I love you. Tell your mother——" He stopped briefly, overcome with emotion. "Tell her I am sorry."

With that last word, he was gone. There was nothing left but memories. I fell to the ground on my knees in shock and sadness. For the first time in my life, I felt completely empty. I sensed the loneness and coldness of depression seeping into my soul. Dad taught me a lesson that day. It was the hardest message of them all.

Nothing lasts forever. The happiness that is thrown our way eventually fades away and dies. It was life. Life is fragile and frail, yet we continue on. This was that very moment that separated the tough ones from the weak. The strength is within us all. With all the pain, realities, disappointments, and hurts that we encounter, we falter, yet in that same instant, the strong get up. We rise.

We move on.

There wasn't enough time to say good-bye to Marcus. I knocked on the door, and there was no answer. When I was beginning to leave, Daphne opened the front door, quickly running out and hugging me tightly. She heard I was leaving and had to say farewell.

"Our culture doesn't have a word for good-bye," she said with tears in her eyes. "It is not in our vocabulary."

I nodded, holding my own tears at bay, and looked back at her house once more.

"I wish you didn't have to leave. Marcus said it would hurt too much to see you."

I let out a tearful sigh.

"So instead of saying good-bye, we say *Chee pesa lacheenee*. It means *Until I see you again*."

I laughed and cried at the same time. "*Chee pesa lacheenee*." I hugged her.

I was happy to see Daphne, but a part of me wished that it was Marcus. What did she mean by it hurt too much to see me? Did he blame me? I wished he would come outside.

"He's not here, Amanda," Daphne said with a slight shrug. "I don't know where he is."

I nodded again in a silent gesture of understanding, and then I got inside the cab, sat down next to Nanny Ivy, and placed my hand on the window. Daphne did the same in return as the car slowly moved away.

As I think back to those days. I wish I had listened to my father's last words.

As I left for my unknown destination with Nanny

and Toby by my side, how was I to know of the events that would come? My hasty judgment and uncontrolled abilities may be my undoing. It may be the very fabric that will make me lose the only things I have left —

Marcus and My Mortal Soul

Marcus gazed through the plain-glass window at the terminal. He watched as the plane took off, flying into the dark night. He placed his left palm on the glass as he positioned his forehead gently on the cold surface. That's how he felt without Amanda. Cold.

He watched until the plane connected to the horizon and slowly disappeared into the night sky above.

"No, Amanda, we're not done here." His blue eyes searched the darkness. "Not yet."

A special thanks to all my family and friends,
especially Lynda; couldn't do it without you.
Your encouragement and support made all this possible.
Love you all.
D. M. Imbordino

CPSIA information can be obtained at www.ICGtesting.com
Printed in the USA
BVOW040352200313

315993BV00001B/2/P

9 781478 714286